Charles Rogers

Life of George Wishart

The Scottish martyr, with his translation of the Helvetian Confession and a

genealogical history of the family of Wishart

Charles Rogers

Life of George Wishart
The Scottish martyr, with his translation of the Helvetian Confession and a
genealogical history of the family of Wishart

ISBN/EAN: 9783337243876

Printed in Europe, USA, Canada, Australia, Japan

Cover: Foto ©Raphael Reischuk / pixelio.de

More available books at **www.hansebooks.com**

LIFE

OF

GEORGE WISHART

THE SCOTTISH MARTYR

WITH HIS

TRANSLATION OF THE HELVETIAN CONFESSION

AND A

GENEALOGICAL HISTORY OF THE FAMILY OF WISHART

BY THE

REV. CHARLES ROGERS, LL.D.

HISTORIOGRAPHER TO THE ROYAL HISTORICAL SOCIETY, FELLOW OF THE SOCIETY
OF ANTIQUARIES OF SCOTLAND, AND CORRESPONDING MEMBER OF THE
HISTORICAL AND GENEALOGICAL SOCIETY OF NEW ENGLAND

EDINBURGH:
WILLIAM PATERSON, PRINCES STREET
1876

EDINBURGH:
PRINTED BY M'FARLANE AND ERSKINE,
ST JAMES SQUARE.

FROM THE MAYOR'S CALENDAR BRISTOL.

PREFACE.

An inquiry into the life of George Wishart presented few attractions. Believing that he claimed the gift of prophecy, Mr Hill Burton * describes him as "a visionary." Mr Froude† charges him with preaching without authority and with illegally assuming the priestly office. Professor Lorimer‡ alleges that, in his early ministry, he denied the doctrine of the Atonement. Mr Tytler § has sought to prove that he intended murder, by conspiring against the life of Cardinal Beaton. Having ventured on the elucidation of his history, I have investigated the charges brought against him, with care and, I trust, impartiality. The result will be found in these pages. Meanwhile I may summarise my deductions, and say that the martyr has, from the inquiry, come forth unstained. He did not claim prophetic powers ; he preached with canonical sanction ; he did not act as a priest or ordained clergyman ; he taught the doctrine of the Atonement throughout his whole ministry ; he did not conspire against Beaton, and if he knew of the conspiracy he condemned it.

I have accompanied the memoir of George Wishart with

* Burton's History of Scotland, Edin., 1873, 12mo, vol. iii., p. 251.
† Froude's History of England, Lond., 1870, vol. iv., p. 177.
‡ Lorimer's Historical Sketch of the Scottish Reformation, Lond., 1860.
§ Tytler's History of Scotland, Edin., 1869, vol. iii., pp. 365-374.

his translation of the first Helvetian Confession. I have added a genealogical history of the House of Wishart, which includes a memoir of Sir John Wishart of Pitarrow.

For useful materials I have been much indebted to Mr J. F. Nicholls, of the City Library, Bristol, the Rev. Dr Struthers, minister of Prestonpans, and Robert R. Stodart, Esq., of the Lyon Office. I also record my indebtedness to the town-clerks of Montrose and Dundee, and to Mr Walter Macleod, of Edinburgh, who, as a professional searcher of the Public Records, cannot be too highly praised.

GRAMPIAN LODGE, FOREST HILL, S.E.
December 1875.

MEMOIR

OF

GEORGE WISHART.

———◆———

DURING the reign of the fifth James, the intolerance of Scottish churchmen had reached its height. The clergy were cruel and rapacious. They seized the chief offices in the State, and the people groaned under their misrule. Feigning charity, they practised avarice. Their lives were dissolute in the extreme. The monasteries, formerly the sanctuaries of religion and letters, had become the unhallowed resorts of unblushing profligacy. Divine worship was a thing of unmeaning pomp and empty ceremony. Sacerdotal oppression crushed the national energies; and with the degradation of the sacred office religion began to be despised. Each confessor, as he arose, was dragged before the ecclesiastical tribunal, and might escape death only by a recantation alike public and degrading. The martyrdom at St Andrews, in 1527, of Patrick Hamilton, nephew of the Earl of Arran, and a descendant of the royal house, sufficiently proved that, in the maintenance of its supremacy, the Roman Church was determined to strike everywhere. But the death of this amiable martyr, instead of repressing, stimulated inquiry, and induced further investigation into the working of a system, maintained by the sale of indulgences on the one hand, and upheld by the executioner on the other.

James Wishart of Pitarrow, Clerk of Justiciary, and King's Advocate in the reign of James IV., married, prior to the 13th

April 1512, as his second wife, Elizabeth Learmont. This gentlewoman was a daughter of Learmont of Balcomie, and sister of that James Learmont, whose name as a statesman we shall find associated with public events in the interest of the Reformation. The family were descended from the older House of Learmont of Ercildoune, or Earlston, in the county of Berwick, of which Thomas the Rhymer was the most conspicuous member.

George Wishart, the future martyr, was the only son of James Wishart of Pitarrow, by his second wife. He was probably called George after his maternal grandfather; the name was certainly derived from his mother's family.* The precise date of his birth is unknown, but it has generally been assigned to the year 1513. By the death of his father, which took place before May 1525, his upbringing would devolve on his mother, assisted probably by her brother, James Learmont of Balcomie.

George Wishart chose the clerical profession, in which several members of his House had attained distinction, and wherein his prospects of advancement, owing to the intimacy which subsisted between his family and David Beaton, Abbot of Arbroath, the future cardinal, were not inconsiderable.† As his name does not occur in the registers of any of the Scottish colleges, it is extremely probable that he was sent by his maternal uncle to one or more of the universities of Germany. During the progress of his studies he seems to have embraced the Reformed doctrines. In the year 1534 John Erskine of Dun established at Montrose a school for the Greek language, under the superintendence of a learned Frenchman.‡ On the retirement of this foreigner, Wishart, who had lately returned from the Continent, took his place. Having imported copies of the Greek Testament, he distri-

---

* George Learmont was, in 1531, infeft as "son and heir of umq¹ James Learmont of Balcomie and Grizel Meldrum."

† See Genealogical History of the Family of Wishart, *infra*.

‡ Life of John Erskine of Dun; Wodrow MSS., vol. i.; Biblioth. Coll., Glasg.

buted them among his pupils. This procedure was reported to John Hepburn, Bishop of Brechin, who summoned him to appear in his diocesan court. This was in 1538.*

The times were perilous. Wishart saw his danger and fled. Proceeding to Cambridge, he entered the College of Bennet or Corpus Christi. Cambridge was a nursery of the Reformed doctrines. There, in the Augustinian monastery of which Barnes was prior, and Coverdale one of the monks, Bilner and Latimer had preached the new faith. There, too, had Cranmer and Ridley read the Scriptures in the original tongues: the former being a Fellow of Jesus College, the latter Master of Pembroke.

Wishart was probably invited to Cambridge by Dr Barnes, with whom he may have contracted an intimacy at Wittenberg, where that eminent divine resided with Luther. At Cambridge he was introduced to Hugh Latimer, Bishop of Worcester. By Latimer his acquaintance would be earnestly cultivated. Each could point to oppression at the hands of bigoted churchmen. During a preaching tour which, under a licence from the University of Cambridge, he undertook in 1531, Latimer, in the pulpits of Bristol, denounced the doctrine of purgatory and the invocation of the saints. His prelections were received with favour by the laity; and on the invitation of the mayor he consented to conduct service on Easter Sunday. Informed of his intention, the local clergy procured an order from the Bishop of Worcester, an Italian named De Ghinuce, prohibiting any clerk from conducting service in the city, without his special sanction. The clergy next accused him of immorality, and as he disproved the charges brought against him, they arraigned him as a heretic in the court of Archbishop Warham. Their prosecution was stopped by the accession of Cranmer to the primacy. Being now bishop of the diocese, which he became in 1535, he was desirous that the Reformed doctrines should be preached in a city where a portion of the laity were willing to receive them, while as bishop he hoped to protect the preacher from molestation.

* Petrie's History of the Catholick Church, part ii., p. 182.

Eager to obey his wishes, and to be useful in the Church as a preacher or evangelist, Wishart agreed to proceed to Bristol.

Obtaining from Latimer orders as *a reader*,* Wishart commenced his labours in Bristol, by lecturing, on Sunday the 15th May 1539, in the church of St Nicholas. The clergy were on the alert. They silenced Latimer eight years before, and in 1525 had compelled Dr Robert Barnes to bear his faggot.† Wishart they pounced upon at once, charging him before the mayor and justices with preaching doctrines condemned by the Church.

Arresting the preacher, the mayor sought direction, as to further procedure, from the Recorder, Lord Cromwell, in the following letter :

"Pleaseth it your honourable Lordship to be advertised that certeyn accusations are made and had by Sir John Kerell,‡ Deane of Bristowe, deputie of the Bishop of Worcester, our ordinary, and dyvers others, inhabitants of Bristowe foresaid, against one Geo. Wischarde, a Scotisheman born, lately beyng before your honourable Lordship ; which accusations the said deane and other inhabitants aforesaid hath presented before me, the Mayor of Bristowe and justices of peace. And the same accusations I have received, sendyng the same unto your said honourable Lordship. And, furthermore, the Chamberlain and the Deane of Bristowe shall sygnyfy unto your honourable Lordship, the very truth in the premysses, unto whom we shall desyre you to give credence. And then our Lord preserve your honourable Lordship in helth and welth, according unto your own hartiest desire.

"At Bristowe the ix. day of June, Anno Regis Henrici VIII. xxxi.

"Be me THOMAS JEFFRYES, *Mayor of Bristol.*

"To the Right Honorable Lord,
    "Lord Pryvy Seale."§

* This was an inferior order in the Church. The reader possessed a faculty to preach, but he was not under the vow of celibacy like ecclesiastics of a higher grade. Wishart is styled "the reader" in the correspondence which follows.

† Seyer's History of Bristol, 1821, 2 vols. 8vo, vol. ii., p. 215.

‡ The name of the dean was Kearne.

§ From the Original in the Public Record Office.

Wishart in the hands of Lord Cromwell was safe. But hostile influences were at work. On Monday the 16th May, the day subsequent to the lecture in St Nicholas' church, the Duke of Norfolk introduced, in the House of Peers, the "Bloody Act of the Six Articles,"* intended to restore Catholic ascendancy, and prove a scourge to those who maintained Protestant sentiments. In June the Act passed both Houses of Parliament, and, receiving the royal assent, became law. Forthwith ecclesiastical courts, assuming the worst features of the Inquisition, began to persecute to extremity those who upheld the new opinions. For refusing to subscribe the articles Bishop Latimer was thrown into prison, and compelled to resign his bishopric. The persecution which overtook him was extended to his *protégé* the reader. An indictment by the Bristol clergy against Wishart, was laid before an ecclesiastical court, consisting of the Primate, Archbishop Cranmer, who still halted between two opinions, Clark, Bishop of Bath, Repps, Bishop of Norwich, and Sampson, Bishop of Chichester. Advised by Cranmer, Wishart consented to retract. Receiving his submission, the court ordained him to carry a faggot in St Nicholas' church, Bristol, on Sunday the 13th July, and in Christ church, of the same city, on the following Sunday.†

The heresy of which Wishart was accused is mentioned in a contemporary record, belonging to the corporation of Bristol, known as the *Mayor's Calendar*. Commenced in 1479 by Robert Riccart, the town-clerk, the record was continued under the direction of the municipal authorities ; it is now preserved among the muniments of the city. Of the entry relating to Wishart, having obtained a photograph, we present a facsimile on the opposite page. It reads thus :

"1639, H. VIII. xxx, Mem.

"That this year the 15th of May a Scott, named George Wysard,

* Froude's History of England, Lond., 1870, vol. iii., pp. 199-217.
† Memoirs, Historical and Biographical, vol. ii., p. 223.

sett furth his lecture in S. Nicholas Church of Bristowe, the moost blasphemous heresy that ever was heard : openly declaryng that Christ nother hathe nor coulde merite for him, ne yett for vs : Which heresy brought many of the Comons of this Towne into a grete Error : and dyvers of theym were persuaded by that heretical lecture to heresy. Whereupon the said stiffeneck'd Scott was accused by Mr John Kerne, Deane of this Diocese of Worc(ester), and soone aft. he was sent to the moost Reverend ffather in God, the Archebishop of Cantrebury, before whom and others, that is to signifie the Bisshops of Bathe, Norwhiche, and Chichestre, w. otheres as Doctors, etc. And he before theym was examined, conuicted and condemned, in and vpon the detestable heresy aboue mentioned. Where-vpon he was injoyned to bere a ffaggott in S. Nicholas Churche forsaid, and the parishe of the same the xiijth day of July as foresaid : And in Christe Churche and parishe therof the xxth day of July abouesaid. Which Iniunction was duely executed in forme forsaid."

Under the belief that the words "Christ nother hathe nor coulde merite for him, ne yett for us," represent the charge brought against the preacher, Mr Seyer, in his "History of Bristol," remarks that Wishart "seems to have adopted notions similar to those which were afterwards brought to a system under the name of Socinianism."* Adopting a similar view of the passage, Professor Lorimer writes :

"It does not admit of a doubt that Wishart had fallen at this early period of his life, while his views of Divine truth were still immature, into some serious misapprehension on the subject of the merits of Christ and the way of human redemption. If the Popish churchmen of Bristol had been his only judges, we might have been justified in receiving, with hesitation, so strange an accusation ; because he was no doubt even then a vigorous opponent of Popish doctrines. And it was probably his zeal in attacking the doctrine of mediatory merit, in the case of the Romish saints, which carried him into the heretical extreme of denying the mediatory merit of the Redeemer himself. But as he was sent up to London to be tried by a tribunal over which Cranmer presided, it is only fair

* Seyer's History of Bristol, vol. ii., p. 223.

to conclude that the sentence which that tribunal pronounced upon him was just."*

These conclusions are unwarranted. As Wishart preached at Bristol under the sanction of Bishop Latimer, it may surely be assumed that his doctrines did not materially differ from those of his patron. And the charge of Socinianism is further rebutted in words which he used in translating the Helvetian Confession not long afterwards. That translation contains the following sentence :

"As he [Christ] onely is our mediatour and intercessour, hoste and sacrifice, byshop lord and our kynge, also do we acknowledge and confesse him onely to be our attonement and ransome, satisfaction, expiacion ; our wisdome, our defence, and our onely deliuerer ; refusyng utterly all other meanes of lyfe and saluacion, except thus by Chryst onely."

In the interval between quitting intercourse with Latimer —immediately before his visit to Bristol—and his living on the Continent soon after that visit, was Wishart likely to deny the fundamental doctrines of Protestant theology? Does the statement of the Bristol chronicler warrant so improbable a conclusion? Read in their present form, the words descriptive of Wishart's teaching are confused and meaningless. In asserting the general proposition that Christ's merit availed not for others, was he likely to strengthen the affirmation by a special allusion to himself? A chief error of the Romish Church, against which the early English Reformers preached, was the worship of the Virgin. By inserting the word *mother* before "nother" in the record, the passage obtains an intelligibility which it at present lacks. Thus : "George Wysard sett furth his lecture, in S. Nicholas Church of Bristowe, the moost blasphemous heresy that ever was heard ; openly declaryng that Christ [mother] nother hathe nor coulde merite for him, ne yett for vs." Finding, in im-

* The Scottish Reformation : An Historical Sketch, by Dr Peter Lorimer, Lond., 1860, pp. 92-96.

mediate juxtaposition, two words similar in form, as are
mother and nother, the engrossing clerk had inadvertently
omitted one of them, a species of error into which transcribers
are prone to fall. Had the preacher affirmed, as part of his
creed, that the Redeemer's merit did not extend to himself
personally, the Romish clergy would probably have permitted
this portion of his doctrine to pass uncondemned. But
Wishart certainly taught that the Virgin mother had no
merit either for her Divine Son, or for any others.

In connection with Wishart's persecution at Bristol, three
remarkable letters are preserved in the Cottonian MSS.*
These letters have different signatures, but are all evidently
written by one person who, residing at Bristol, was intimately
conversant with the habits and peculiarities of the leading
citizens. With the signature of William Ryppe, the following
letter bears to be despatched from Coventry to Thomas
White in Bread Street, Bristol :

"'Grace and pece be with us.'

"O yow enemys to godes worde, why hath yow accused the
same yong faithfull man that dyd rede the lecto[r] the very worde of
god, he dyd no thing but scripture wold bere hym, and to discharge his conscience? Thowgh the kynge and his counsell, w. his
clergy hath made suche ordynance, yet they that be lerned will leve
the kynges ordinance & styk to the ordinance of god, which is
the Kyng of all Kynges. And we be bounde to dy in god quarell
and leve the ordinance of man, and there this good yong man is
trobelid; but I trust yow shall all repent hit shortly, when my lord
privy seale† do heare of it. And yow folys mayer, and that knave

---

* Brit. Mus., Cotton MSS., Cleopatra EV., fol. 390.

† The celebrated Thomas Cromwell, Earl of Essex, who held office as Recorder
of Bristol, was also Keeper of the Privy Seal. In the books of the city chamberlain is the following entry, respecting a balance of salary due to Lord Essex at the
time of his execution : "For so much the £20 charged in this side, paid to the
Lord of Essex, late Recorder of this town, for his fee due to him at the feast of the
Nativity of our Lord God in Anno 1540 : which customary used to be paid at one
time : and for that the said Lord of Essex was beheaded before that feast in the
same year, anno 1540, we, the auditors, find that the £20 ought not to be allowed
in this account."

Thomas White, w. the lyar Abynton,* the prater Pacy,† & flatering
Hutton,‡ & Dronkyn Tonell,§ folis Coke,‖ dremy Smyth,¶ & the
nigarde Thorne, ** hasty Sylke,†† stuttyng Elyott,‡‡ symple Hart,§§
& grynning Pryn,‖‖ prowde Addamys,¶¶ & pore Woddus,*** the
sturdy parson of saynt Stevyns, the prowde Vicar of saynt Lenardes,
the lying parson of saynt Jonys,††† the dronken parson of saynt
Eweens,‡‡‡ the brayling wrᵣ of the calenders, the prating Vikar of

* The Abyndons were an old Bristol family. Henry Abyndon, Bachelor of
Music at Cambridge in 1463, was a member of King's Chapel, and Master of St
Catherine's Hospital, Brightbow, Bedminster. In 1550 there is mention of
"Abyndon ys Inne." This inn was rebuilt before 1565, and was then known as
the new inn. The individual mentioned in the letter was probably Richard Abyndon, who was mayor of Bristol in 1526, and again in 1537. In 1529 he was
elected M.P. In an old calendar of the city, the following entry occurs : "On
the 17th of July there was such thundering and lightening which lasted from 8
o' the clock at night untill 4 next morning, which was fearfull for to heare ; but
when Richard Abbingdon deceased the thunder also ceased presently."

† "The prater Pacy" was probably the vicar of All-Hallows ; but a person
of the name was mayor of Bristol in 1532.

‡ Hutton cannot be identified.   § Tonnell was mayor of Bristol in 1529.

‖ Coke was mayor in 1535, and M.P. in 1537.

¶ Smyth was sheriff of Bristol in 1533.

** Nicholas Thorne was a wealthy shipowner, and founder of a school at Bristol.
He served as sheriff in 1529. In 1537 he represented the borough in Parliament,
and in 1545 was elected mayor. He died August 19th, 1546. His portrait by
Holbein is extant.

†† A person named Sylke was sheriff of Bristol in 1530; and the "proude vicar
of St Leonards" was also Thomas Sylke. Both belonged to an old Bristol family
of the name. William Sylke was rector of All-Hallows in 1264, when "Isonde,
relict of Hugh Calvestone, grants lands to the Church, on payment of a yearly
rent of a penny or a pair of gloves at her option." By another deed, dated about
the same period, William Sylke "gives, grants, and confirms in fee, for the souls
of his father, John Sylke, his mother, Isabella, and all his predecessors and successors," money "to keep a lamp for ever burning in the church of All-Hallows"
—the said money to be derived from land in Seatepull Street, Bristol. In 1547
a Mrs Sylke bequeathed to the poor of St Thomas's parish three shillings for
annual distribution.

‡‡ Robert Ellyott was sheriff of Bristol in 1522, mayor in 1541, and M.P. in
1542. In the patents of 1501 and 1502, for the discovery and settlement of the
lands in America, his father, Hugh Ellyott, was associated with Ward, Ashe-
hurst, Thomas, and Thorne, merchants of Bristol.

§§ Hart was sheriff of Bristol in 1536.   ‖‖ Pryn was sheriff in 1537.

¶¶ Addamys was mayor of Bristol in 1546.

*** Woddus was sheriff of Bristol in 1535.

††† Thomas Tasker.   ‡‡‡ Waterhouse.

allhalowys, w. dyvers other knave preistes, shall all repent this doing.   Farewell the enemys of the worde of god.

> " Writen in haste at the noble cyty of Coleyn by yo᙮ loviar
> William Ryppe of Brystow."

(*Inserted on the margin.*)

" The worshipfull m᙮ Thomas White in Bredestrete
in Bristow this letter be delyvered w. spede from
Coventre."

The second letter bears to have been written at Rome, by Thomas Abynton.   It is addressed on the margin :

" To the worshipfull m᙮ Thomas Abynton,
in Bristow, this letter be delyvered from
Croydyn to Bristow."

The letter proceeds :

> " Yet onys agayne to the enemys of godes worde as ye knave
> the mayer, very fole to the kynges grace, & enemys to my
> lorde pryvy seale, and to y᙮ awne sell.

> " O yow knavys and enemys to the worde of god now yow
> may se what cruelty yow dyd use in putting this faithfull Reder in
> pryson, and now be glad to putt hym owt agayne : If yow had not
> yow sholde have bene burned owt of yo᙮ howsyng, yow shall repent
> this doing iff some of us do lyve, and specially some of the knave
> preists : as the same prowde knave the Vykar of saynt Leonardes,*
> rowling his night cappe of velvett every day and not able to chaunge
> a man agrote, & the dronken parson of saynt Jonys,† & that per-
> petuall knave the parson of saynt Stevyns, & brasyn face knave of
> allhalows, baburlyppe knave the preist of saynt Leonardes, w. long
> syr harry, and lytle S᙮ Thomas, w. the vycar of saynt Austens, the
> olde fole.   All these of this diocese that have cure shall go lyke
> knavys to sing *Ave regina* when the byshoope cum,‡ for they have
> warning the last visitacion, & take this my warning yow knavys all.
> Now to the Temporalty.   That same knave Thomas Whyte now doth

---

* Thomas Sylke was vicar of St Leonards.   † Thomas Tasker.
‡ Bishop Richard, who was employed as a royal commissioner at Bristol for the surrender of the monastery.

begyn to shrynke in his harnys, but that shall not helpe hym.   And
the folishe mayer must folow a many of knavys counsell, & at the
instance of the two poticarys,* the false knavys that ever was Schrevys
this mr yere, and wily knavys, but they shall smart for this yere,
And that flatering Hutton, and dronken Pacy & false towne-
clerke.† Also the knavys do loke for the suttyll Recorder, but when
he come if he do not holde wt the trew worde of god, my lorde
pryvy seale shall bydd hym walke lyke a knave as he is.   Therefore
I do advyse yow, be ware and discharge the suretyes of the Reader
by tyme : or els yow will repent hitt for he shall make as many as
xx{ty} of you if nede do requyre.   Fare yow well all yow knavys all
that do holde agaynst the same honest man the reader, for he doth
regard the kyng of hevyn before the kyng of England.   And thus
fare yow well yow shall knowe more of my mynde when o{r} byshopp
come from London.

  " Yor lovyer and frende Thomas Abynton in all haste from
  Rome the xth day of January."

The third letter is addressed to Thomas Sylke, Vicar of St
Leonards ; and as the writer demands that the reader should
be set free before the bishop was informed of his detention,
it was probably the first written.

  " To the stynkyng knave Sylke, Vykar of saynt Leonardes.

  " Thow stynkyng knave, I cast in a letter of late into thy
chamber to delyver to the lying knave Thomas or Richard
Abyngton, but thow, lyke a knave, must delyver the letter to that
knave Thomas Whyte.   Be sure thow shalt lese one day one of thy
eares, & that ere it be myddell lent sonday.   Remember my sayng,
I do write unto yow after a charitable maner that yow may delyver the reader ere the Byshoppe do knowe of it.   For when he do
heare of it he will ruffyll amonges yow for it.   The knave Shrevys be

---

 * One of these two apothecaries was David Harris.   He was sheriff in 1539, and
mayor in 1551.   When Richard Sharp was suffering at the stake for heresy, in
1557, he was encouraged by one Thomas Hale, a shoemaker.   This act so enraged
Alderman Harris that he had Hale seized in his bed, and committed to Newgate ;
he was afterwards condemned and burned.   When Queen Elizabeth visited Bristol in 1573, David Harris was ejected from the office of alderman.   The other
" poticary " was probably a relative.

 † The town-clerk was John Colys.

a greate occasion of the same pore man the readers trowble, and
specially that knave Harrye, the potecary.   There is a nother knave
Harrys * in towne, & that a pryvy and wily knave as ever lyved,
crafty and suttyll, and a greate enemy to the worde of god : but
when the Byshoppe do come, he shall handle hym in his kynde ;
thowgh that the same knave Nicoll Thorne † do faver hym, he shall
not helpe hym, nother that ypocrite his wife also.   O yow hard-
harted knavys that will not faver the worde of god, when such
a faithfull yong man dyd take paynes to reade the trew worde of
god and yow to trowble hym for his laboͬ.   May not yow be sory ?
yes trewly.   And if yow had not delyvered hym owt of pryson the
rather, he shold have come owt spyte of yo͘ teth ; like knavys as yow
be all discharge his suretys, I will advise yow.   Say not but yow have
warning.   For if the Poyntmakers ‡ do ryse, some of yow will lese
theyre eares and that shortly.   I understande yow will do no thing
tyll the knave Recorder do come.   I do not mene my good lord
pryvy seale.   I do not call hym knave ; but I call Davy Broke §
knave and gorbely knave, and that droncken Gervys,‖ that lubber
Antony Payne,¶ & slovyn William Yong,** and that dobyll knave
William Chester.††   For sometymes he is w. us and sometymes w.
the knaves, but he shalbe a long knave for it, & his wife a folishe
drabbe for she is the enemy of goddes worde.   Fare yow well for
his tyme, yo͘ loving frende the goodman parson of saynt Stevyns, in
Bedmyster, besydes the kynges towne of Faterford, commende me
to all the knave preistes that be the enemys of goddes worde.   For
if we lyve & the byshoppe together, they shall not trowble this
towne except the kynge do fayle us.   For the knavys have no lern-
ing nor none will lerne.   Yet onys again fare yow well.

   " By yo͘ lovyer David Harrys, poticary, & that scalde knave
        William Fay, from the port of saynt Mary.

   "Commende me to that grynnyng knave the false towne clerke,

---

* Rector of the grammar school.   † Nicholas Thorn.
‡ The pointmakers were a flourishing guild at Bristol.
§ David Broke was mayor of the city in 1527.   ‖ Gervys was sheriff in 1526.
¶ Antony Payne was sheriff in 1534.   ** William Yong was mayor in 1540.
†† William Chester was mayor in 1538.   In the following year he obtained
a grant of the site of the Blackfriars monastery.   When in May 1549 there was an
insurrection in the city, under Pykes' mayoralty, he appeared for the malcontents,
and obtained a pardon for them from Edward VI.

he shall repent other thinges, yow knowe what I meane. Commende me to old folishe Sprynge,* & to the angry Pykes,† w. dyvers other which do not come to my mynde now, but another tyme beware mo of yow."

Having, by burning his faggot, escaped death as the result of his evangelical labours at Bristol, Wishart proceeded to the Continent. According to Bishop Lesley, his contemporary, "he remained long in Germany."‡ In defending himself during his trial at St Andrews he referred to his having sailed on the Rhine ; and as he translated into English the first Confession of the Helvetian Churches, it is probable that he visited Switzerland. In 1542 he returned to Cambridge, and there sought employment as a tutor. Respecting this portion of his career, we obtain the following particulars in a communication made to Foxe, the martyrologist, by Emery Tylney, one of his pupils :

"About the yeare of our Lord, a thousand, five hundreth, fortie and three, there was, in the universitie of Cambridge, one Maister George Wischart, commonly called Maister George of Bennet's Colledge, who was a man of tall stature, polde headed, and on the same a French cap of the best. Judged of melancholye complexion by his phsiognomie, blacke haired, long bearded, comely of personage, well spoken after his country of Scotland, courteous, lowly, lovely, glad to teach, desirous to learne, and was well trauelled, hauing on him for his habit or clothing, neuer but a mantell frise gowne to the shoes, a blacke Millian fustain dublet, and plaine blacke hosen, course new canuasse for his shirtes, and white falling bandes and cuffes at the handes. All the which apparell, he gaue to the poore, some weekly, some monethly, some quarterly as hee liked, sauing his Frenche cappe, which hee kept the whole yeare of my beeing with him. Hee was a man modest, temperate, fearing God, hating couctousnesse, for his charitie had neuer ende, nighte, morne, nor daye, hee forbare one meale in three, one day in foure for the most part, except something to comfort nature. Hee lay hard upon a pouffe of

---

* Mayor in 1540.   † Sheriff in 1533.
‡ Lesley's History of Scotland, Edin., 1838, p. 191.

straw, course new canuasse sheetes, which, when he change, he gaue away. He had commonly by his bedside a tubbe of water, in the which (his people being in bed, the candle put out, and all quiet) hee used to bathe himselfe, as I being very yong, being assured offen heard him, and in one light night discerned him; hee loved me tenderly, and I him, for my age, as effectually. Hee taught with great modestie and grauitie, so that some of his people thought him seuere, and would haue slain him, but the Lord was his defence. And hee, after due correction for their malice, by good exhortation amended them, and hee went his way. O that the Lord had left him to mee his poore boy, that he might haue finished that hee had begunne! For in his Religion hee was as you see heere in the rest of his life, when he went into Scotland with diuers of the Nobilitie, that came for a treaty to King Henry the eight. His learning was no less sufficient, than his desire, alwayes prest and readie to do good in that hee was able both in the house priuately, and in the schoole publickely, professing and reading diuers authours.

"If I should declare his love to mee and all men, his charitie to the poore, in giuing, relieuing, caring, helping, prouiding, yea infinitely stu lying how to do good unto all, and hurt to none, I should sooner want words than just cause to commend him.

"All this I testifie with my whole heart and trueth of this godly man. Hee that made all, gouerneth all, and shall judge all, knoweth I speake the truthe, that the simple may be satisfied, the arrogant confounded, the hypocrite disclosed.   EMERY TYLNEY." *

To complete the long-pending negotiations with the English Government for the marriage of Edward Prince of Wales with the infant Queen Mary, commissioners from Scotland proceeded to London in June 1543. These commissioners were the Earl of Glencairn, Sir George Douglas, Sir William Hamilton of Sanquhar, James Learmont of Balcomie, and Henry Balnaves. They met the English commissioners at Greenwich on the 1st of July, when the marriage treaty was settled, and certain differences between the countries amicably adjusted.† When the commissioners left Scot-

---

* Foxe's Acts and Monuments, ed. 1596, p. 1155.
† Rymer's Fœdera, vol. xiv., pp. 786-791.

land, the governor Arran, then a professor of the Reformed faith, was at variance with Cardinal Beaton ; and as no reconciliation between them seemed probable, Learmont of Balcomie regarded the season as especially suitable for his relative leaving Cambridge and returning to the north. Accepting his counsel, Wishart joined the commissioners, and accompanied them to Scotland, which they reached before the 31st of July.*

Wishart intended at once to enter upon the duties of an evangelist. But the altered condition of public affairs rendered such a proceeding absolutely dangerous. Beaton had regained his authority, and the weak governor, in becoming reconciled to him, evidenced a desire to perpetuate his friendship by publicly abjuring the Reformed faith.

Amidst the perils of the time, Wishart found a retreat in his native home, the mansion of Pitarrow.† There he remained from July 1543 till the spring of 1545, dividing his time between the study of theology and the cultivation of the arts. When the old mansion of Pitarrow was being demolished in 1802,‡ the workmen laid open, under the wainscoting which covered the walls of the great hall, a series of well executed paintings.

These paintings were in bright colours. One over the fireplace represented the Pope on horseback, attended by a company of cardinals, uncovered. In front stood a white palfrey, richly caparisoned, held by a person in elegant apparel. Beyond was the Cathedral of St Peter, of which the doors were open, as if to receive the procession. Under the painting were these lines :

* Sadler's State Papers, vol. i., pp. 235, 242-245. Knox, who mentions Wishart's return to Scotland with the commissioners, erroneously states that the event took place in 1544 (Knox's History, ed. 1846, vol. i., p. 102).

† Pitarrow is situated in a rural district, fifteen miles from Montrose, on the east coast of Forfarshire.

‡ Dr George Cook's History of the Scottish Reformation, vol. i., p. 272 ; New Statistical Account, Kincardineshire, p. 81.

"In Papam.
"Laus tua non tua fraus: virtus, non gloria rerum
Scandere te fecit hoc decus eximium.
Dat sua pauperibus gratis nec munera curat
Curia Papalis quod more percipimus.
Hae carmina potuis legenda cancros imitando."

Literally rendered, the inscription reads:

"Thy merit, not thy craft; thy worth, not thy ambition, raised thee to this pitch of eminence. The Papal Curia, as we well know, gives freely to the poor, nor grudges its gifts."

But as the writer informs us his verses are to be read by imitating crabs—that is, backwards—a very different meaning is derived—thus:

"The Papal Curia, as we well know, grudges its gifts, nor bestows on the poor freely. To this pitch of eminence thy ambition raised thee, not thy worth; thy craft, not thy merit."

Knox writes: "Wishart excelled in all human science."[*] During his first residence in Germany he may have acquired the art of painting, and he might have studied under Holbein. The brilliancy of colour apparent in the Pitarrow paintings would certainly assign them to an artist of the German school. To the narrative of Wishart's character, supplied to Foxe, Tylney adds these lines, which he styles:

"DOGMATA EJUSDEM GEORGII.

"Fides sola sine operibus justificat;
Opera ostendunt et ostentant fidem;
Romana ecclesia putativé caput mundi,
Lex canonica caput Papæ,
Missæ ministerium, mysterium iniquitatis."[†]

There is here, as in the lines on the painting at Pitarrow, a double meaning. This bipartite arrangement is intended:

---

* Knox's History, ed. 1846, vol. i., p. 125.
† Foxe's Acts and Monuments, ed. 1596, p. 1155.

```
" Fides sola  . . . . . . .  sine operibus justificat
Opera ostendunt et ostentant  .  fidem
Romana ecclesia  . . . . .  putativé caput mundi
Lex canonica  . . . . . .  caput Papæ
Missæ ministerium  . . . .  mysterium iniquitatis."
```

In the first division, Rome asserts : " This is the one faith. The Roman Church, the canon law, the service of the mass, prove and show good works." In the other, the preacher presents his confession : " Papal supremacy, that mystery of iniquity, which thinks itself the head of the world, justifies faith without works."

It would be rash to affirm that a similarity of manner and sentiment, striking as it certainly is, proves that the *dogmata* and the Pitarrow inscription proceeded from the same pen. But the assertion will be allowed, that George Wishart, who wrote the *dogmata*, translated the Helvetian Confession, and died in testimony of his hatred of Romish error, might have composed an inscription in his paternal mansion which condemned the Papacy. Such an inscription he was more likely to compose than any other member of his House whose history is known. And if he inscribed his ancestral hall with his pen, may he not likewise have adorned it with his brush? Who more likely to illustrate a painting than the painter himself? The paintings at Pitarrow were executed on the plastered wall ; the wainscoting which afterwards concealed them was introduced subsequent to Wishart's period.

Tired of his prolonged seclusion at Pitarrow, Wishart determined to resume his duties as an evangelist. In reading the Scriptures to the people in their native tongue, he had the authority of the State,[*] and being in reader's orders, he possessed as an instructor the sanction of the Church. Renting a house at Montrose, the " next unto the church except one,"[†] he there read and explained the Scriptures to all who

[*] An Act of the Estates was proclaimed on the 19th March 1543, declaring that it should be lawful for all men to read the Old and New Testaments in the mother tongue, and providing that " no man preach to the contrary upon pain of death."

[†] Knox's History, ed. 1846, vol. i., p. 125; Petrie's History of the Catholick Church, Hague, 1662, folio, p. 182.

came. After a time he removed to Dundee, where he publicly read and expounded the Epistle to the Romans. His
prelections, conducted within eleven miles of the Castle of
St Andrews, could not long escape the notice of Cardinal
Beaton, who, since his reconciliation with the governor, possessed an authority nearly absolute. The cardinal might not
prevent the reading of the Scriptures; he might not close, save
on a specific charge, a mouth opened by the Church. But
one who is disposed to persecute may readily find excuse to
justify his interference. Charging Wishart with convoking
the lieges without the royal sanction, he procured from the
queen regent and the governor a proclamation, calling on
him to desist. By one Robert Mill, a magistrate of Dundee, who had professed the Reformed doctrines, but had
lately abjured them, the proclamation was handed to the
preacher as he conducted service. " He remained," writes
Knox, " a little space with his eyes bent towards heaven, and
thereafter looking sorrowfully to the speaker and the people,
said : God is witness that I never intended your trouble but
your comfort. Yea, your trouble is more dolorous to me
than it is to yourselves. But I am assured that to refuse
God's Word, and to chase from you His messengers, shall not
preserve you from trouble, but it shall bring you into it. For
God shall send to you messengers who will not be afraid of
horning * nor yet banishment. I have offered unto you the
Word of Salvation, and with the hazard of my life I have
remained among you. Now ye yourselves refuse me, and
therefore must I leave my innocence to be declared by God.
If it be long prosperous with you, I am not led by the Spirit of
Truth ; but if unlooked-for trouble apprehend you, acknowledge the cause and turn to God, for He is merciful." †
     Among those present when Mill served the proclamation
was the Earl Marischal, ‡ who entreated the preacher to dis-

---

* Putting to the horn, i.e., being denounced a rebel. This menace would, as
matter of course, be contained in the proclamation.
     † Knox's History, Edin., 1846, vol. i., pp. 125, 126.
     ‡ By Sir Ralph Sadler, in a report to Henry VIII., dated 27th March 1543, the

regard it, or to accompany him to the north and there prose-
cute his ministry. But Wishart had promised to the Earl of
Glencairn* that he would next preach in Ayrshire, and he proceeded thither at once.

Ayrshire was included in the see of Glasgow, and Gavin
Dunbar, the archbishop, was determined to check in his diocese the spread of heretical opinions. Informed that Wishart
was preaching in Ayr, he went there with a body of attendants, and took possession of the church. Lord Glencairn and
George Crawfurd of Loch Norris,† attended by their vassals,
also proceeded thither to defend the preacher. But Wishart
discommended violence. He invited the people to accompany
him to the market cross, where, writes Knox, " he made so
notable a sermon that his very enemies themselves were confounded." Dunbar preached in the parish church which he
had usurped. Inexpert in public teaching, he commended
his office, and promised a more edifying discourse on his
return.‡

Wishart prosecuted his labours chiefly in the district of
Kyle. For a time he occupied the parish church of Galston,
under the protection of John Lockhart of Barr, a Protestant
landowner.§ Invited to preach at Mauchline, an adjoining
parish, he consented ; but the use of the church was resisted
on the plea that an elegant shrine preserved in it might be

Earl Marischal is described as "a goodly young gentleman, well given to his
Majesty." He was very friendly to the Reformation. During the civil wars in
the reign of Queen Mary he shut himself in his Castle of Dunottar, and consequently became known as William of the Tower. He died about the year 1581
(Sadler's State Papers, vol. i., p. 126).

* William Cunningham, fourth Earl of Glencairn, was in 1526 appointed Lord
High Treasurer. He early attached himself to the Reformers, and bore a conspicuous part in their early struggles ; he died in 1547. His son Alexander, fifth
earl, is historically known as " the good earl."

† Now called Dumfries House, a seat of the Marquess of Bute.

‡ Knox's History, Edin., 1846, vol. i., p. 127.

§ John Lockhart of Barr is, in a legal instrument dated Glasgow, 20th November 1510, nominated procurator and assignee of Mr Patrick Shaw, Vicar of Monk-
town, about to set out for Rome. He is noticed in the rental book of the diocese
of Glasgow in 1553 (Diocesan Registers of Glasgow, vol. i., p. 151; vol. ii.,
p. 381).

injured by the populace. Among the opposers were George
Campbell of Monkgarswood, Mungo Campbell of Brounside,
and George Read of Tempilland. At their instance, Sir Hugh
Campbell of Loudoun, sheriff of the county, prohibited the use
of the church, and caused the doors to be watched by a civic
guard. This procedure was obnoxious to an influential landowner, Hew Campbell of Kinzeancleugh,* who, with his
friends and followers, sought to overpower the guard and
enter the edifice by force. Wishart dissuaded Campbell from
exciting public strife. "Brother," said he, "Christ Jesus is as
potent in the fields as in the kirk. He himself oftener
preached on the mountain, in the desert, and at the seaside,
than in the temple. God sends by me the Word of Peace,
and the blood of no man must be shed this day for the preaching of it." Having calmed his friend's vehemence, Wishart
proceeded to a meadow, and there from a stone fence preached
to an eager crowd. His discourse lasted three hours. It was
attended by the conversion of Laurence Rankin, the laird of
Sheill, a man whose corrupt life had been notorious.†

Under the protection of the Earls of Cassilis ‡ and Glencairn, and others, Wishart had preached in Ayrshire about four
weeks, when he was recalled to Dundee. A terrible epidemic
had broken out in the place four days § after his departure,
and his return was urgently entreated. A contemporary
chronicler informs us that in August 1545 a fatal pestilence
visited all the burghs of Scotland.‖ In that month it is probable Wishart returned to Dundee. His departure from Kyle
grieved many who had become attached to his ministry. To

---

* Hew Campbell of Kinzeancleugh was a cadet of the House of Loudoun. His
son, Robert Campbell of Kinzeancleugh, was a zealous friend of John Knox and
a devoted promoter of the Reformation.

† Knox's History, edit. 1846, vol. i., p. 128.

‡ Gilbert Kennedy, third Earl of Cassilis, was taken prisoner at the battle of
Solway, and consequently became known to Henry VIII., who held him in high
esteem. He was a vigorous upholder of the Protestant cause.

§ Spottiswoode's History of the Church of Scotland, Edin., 1851, 8vo, vol. i.,
p. 151.

‖ Diurnal of Occurrents, Maitland Club, p. 39.

their entreaties that he would remain among them, he replied that his former hearers " were in trouble and needed comfort ;" he added : " Perhaps the hand of God will cause them now to revere that Word which formerly, through fear of man, they lightly esteemed."*

At Dundee, on his return, Wishart excited a deep interest. Those who remembered his words when the apostate Mill interrupted his preaching, hoped that the pestilence which had followed so closely his departure might be arrested on his return.   He was urged to resume his public ministrations, but as those who attended the sick or exhibited symptoms of ailment were carefully avoided, there was difficulty in arranging matters. Wishart proposed to preach from the East Port, the sick and suspected being accommodated without, and those in health within the walls.† The proposal was accepted, and the preacher discoursed from the 20th verse of the 107th Psalm : " He sent His Word and healed them." He set forth the blessed nature of Holy Scripture, and the comfort which it brought to the bereaved. Afflictive dispensations, he remarked, conduced to humility and repentance. The Divine mercy, he said, was alike manifest in seasons of adversity and sickness as in times of prosperity and health. Affliction was a great teacher, and God frequently removed His friends from troubles which were to come. The preacher enjoined a faithful attendance on the sick, and exhorted that prayer should accompany the means used for their recovery. The hearers were deeply moved, and retired with expressions of thankfulness. ‡

At Dundee Wishart preached frequently, and also waited upon the sick. His proceedings were again reported to the cardinal, who now had recourse to an assassin. John Wighton, a priest belonging to Dundee, undertook to destroy the

* Knox's History, edit. 1846, vol. i., p. 129.

† At this time the town of Dundee was surrounded by a double wall, with ports or gates, which were removed about the end of the eighteenth century, except the East Gate, or Cowgate Port, which, out of respect to Wishart's memory, has been preserved.

‡ Knox's Works, edit. 1846, vol. i., p. 130.

preacher. Armed with a dagger, he entered the place of worship in which Wishart was discoursing, and, concealing himself behind the pulpit, waited his descent. Happily, Wishart remarked his presence, and before he had time to strike, seized him fast. "What would you do, my friend?" said the preacher, calmly. Dreading instant death, Wighton threw himself on his knees and entreated mercy. The congregation had retired, but a few persons who remained behind gave the alarm, and a crowd burst upon the scene. "Let us smite the traitor!" shouted a multitude of voices. Wishart remarked that he was unhurt, and begged that the aggressor might be spared. "He who touches him will trouble me," he said earnestly. He then improved the occasion by pointing out the perils which attend the Christian in his pilgrimage, and after duly exhorting his intended murderer, secured his retreat.*

Wishart remained in Dundee till the pestilence had ceased. From Lords Cassilis and Glencairn he received letters intimating that a provincial Synod of the Church was to meet at Edinburgh on the 13th January, and promising him a public audience on the occasion. He was pleased with this proposal, and agreeing to be at Edinburgh in January, remarked that having "finished one battle he was ready for another." Meanwhile he proceeded to Montrose, where he occasionally preached.

Having failed to silence the preacher by the dagger of the assassin, Beaton devised a stratagem for his arrest. At Montrose Wishart was waited upon by a jaded messenger, who thrust a letter into his hand. The letter bore that his friend John Kinnear of Kinnear, in Fife,† lay dangerously sick, and desired to see him at once. Moved by affection, Wishart mounted a led horse brought by the messenger, and in the company of a few friends proceeded on his journey. Having passed the outskirts of the town, he remarked to his com-

---

* Knox's Works, edit. 1846, vol. i., p. 131.

† John Kynnear of Kynnear in the parish of Kilmany, Fifeshire, was, on the 30th July 1543, served heir to his father, David Kynnear de eodem, in the lands and barony of Kynnear (Inq. Spec., Fife, No. 2).

panions that he began to suspect treachery. Some of his attendants riding forward discovered, at a retired and sheltered spot, a troop of about sixty horsemen, evidently waiting an arrival. The preacher and his friends returned to Montrose.*

About the end of November Wishart proposed to leave Montrose for Edinburgh. By his early friend, John Erskine of Dun, he was urged to remain in retirement, but he remarked that he could not break his promise. Having reached Dundee, he was from thence conducted to Invergowrie, a hamlet in the vicinity, where he was entertained at the house of James Watson, one of his converts. Knox relates an anecdote in connection with this visit. The preacher rose during the night, and proceeding to a secluded portion of the garden, there expressed himself as if in pain, and afterwards knelt down and engaged in prayer. Two members of the household, who chanced to be awake, observed his procedure, and followed him unseen. Informing him next morning that they had remarked his vigil, they begged an explanation. He answered that he believed his life would be a short one. Knox regards this occurrence as evidence that the preacher was supernaturally informed of his approaching martyrdom. Such a view was not unnatural in times of superstition. But Wishart's act is easily explained. He evidently suffered from an imperfect circulation, which, as in the case of the Scottish poet, Robert Burns, induced at night strong fever, or unnatural warmth. Tylney relates that at Cambridge he had "commonly by his bedside a tub of water, in the which, his people being in bed, the candle put out, and all quiet, he used to bathe himself." It was, doubtless, while suffering from a feverish attack to which he was subject that he sought relief in the coolness of the garden. These attacks becoming probably more frequent and severe, led him to say to those who rashly questioned him, that he feared his life would not be prolonged.

From Invergowrie Wishart proceeded to Perth, then desig-

* Knox's History, ed. 1846, vol. i., p. 132.

nated St Johnstone. He adopted this circuitous route to
Edinburgh in order to avoid the nearer but more dangerous road through the eastern district of Fife, where the cardinal maintained a nearly absolute jurisdiction. Travelling
from Perth by way of Kinross, he reached the ferry at King-
horn, and thence crossed the Forth to Leith, the port of
Edinburgh. It was the beginning of December, and he expected that the Earls of Cassilis and Glencairn would be
in the capital awaiting his arrival. As they had not come,
he was by friendly persons advised to remain in tempor-
ary concealment. He acquiesced, but soon complained of
the restraint. "Wherein do I differ from one dead," he
exclaimed, "except that I eat and drink? Hitherto God
has accepted my labours for the instruction of the ignorant and the exposure of error. Now I lurk in secret as one
who is ashamed." Entreating that he might be permitted to
resume his ministry, arrangements were made accordingly.
On the second Sunday of December he preached at Leith,
selecting as his subject the Parable of the Sower. The bold-
ness of his teaching increased the alarm of his friends, who,
believing a report that the governor and the cardinal were
to be in Edinburgh shortly, begged that he would quit so
dangerous a vicinity.[*]

At this period Wishart was introduced to three conspicuous
opponents of the Romish Church, Alexander Crichton of
Brunstone, Hugh Douglas of Longniddry, and John Cockburn of Ormiston. Subsequent to his public appearance at
Leith, these persons entertained him at their houses, and
instituted arrangements for his safety. Intimately associated with him, as they became, during the last and most
eventful period of his ministry, they severally claim particular notice. Crichton of Brunstone had hitherto been
a supporter of the Reformed cause, rather from hostility
to Beaton than from any absolute conviction. His policy
had been singularly vacillating. In 1539 he was, as one
of his confidential friends, despatched by Cardinal Beaton

* Knox's History, ed. 1846, vol. i., p. 134.

with letters to the court of Rome. Having quarrelled with the
cardinal, he attached himself to Arran,* who employed him
on diplomatic missions to France and England.† But renouncing the governor's favour, he made himself known to
Sir Ralph Sadler, through whom he was recommended to the
English court. The history of his negotiations with Henry
VIII. for the destruction of the cardinal will be detailed afterwards. But it is worthy of remark that subsequent to his
intercourse with Wishart his name no longer appears on the
list of conspirators. His latter history may be related briefly.
In 1548 he was forfeited and escaped from Scotland. He
died before the 5th December 1558, as on that day the process of forfeiture against him was reduced by the Scottish
Parliament at the instance of John Crichton, who is described
as "eldest lawful son and heir of umquhile Alexander Creich-
ton of Brunstane." ‡

Hugh Douglas of Longniddry was a man of firm principle
and strong faith. A scion of the House of Douglas of Dal-
keith, he was an early promoter of the Reformed doctrines.
Under his roof John Knox, after renouncing his priestly office
at Haddington, obtained employment and shelter as tutor to
his sons, Francis and George.§ Knox had resided with Douglas
about eighteen months prior to Wishart's visit, and it is probable that his recommendation of the stranger tended towards
his favourable reception by the Reformers of Haddingtonshire. Of the personal history of Hugh Douglas, apart from
his support of Knox and Wishart, not much is known. His

* Sadler's State Papers, pp. 25, 185, 280.

† On the 8th November 1545, there was paid " be my Lord Gouernouis speciall
command to the Laird of Brounstoun in support of his expenses maid in tyme of
his being in Ingland lauborand for redres of certane Scottis schippis tane be the
Inglische men, &c., 44 lib." (Treasurers' Accounts).

‡ Acta Parl. Scot., vol. ii., p. 520.

§ John Knox was born at Haddington and educated under the learned Mair at
the University of Glasgow. In the protocol books of Haddington his name occurs
in 1540, 1541, and 1542, under the style of "Schir John Knox," the designation of
priests who had not attained the academical rank of master. A notarial instrument of assignment, dated 27th March 1543, bears his subscription as "Minister
of the sacred altar and apostolic notary."

son, Francis Douglas of Longniddry, in a deed of ratification, dated 19th April 1567, is named as third in the line of succession to James, Earl of Morton, failing his male issue.* By Sir George Douglas, a descendant of the House, that portion of the lands of Longniddry which belonged to his family was, in 1650, sold to the Earl of Winton, who also acquired the other portion. The estates of the Earl of Winton, having been forfeited in 1715, were purchased by the York Building Company, by whom they were sold in 1779 to John Glassel, a surgeon, who acquired a fortune by trading in Virginia. His only child became Duchess of Argyll. By her son, the present Duke of Argyll, the lands of Longniddry were sold to the Earl of Wemyss, who guards with pious care an aged tree under which Knox preached. A circular mound covers the foundations of the ancient mansion.

John Cockburn of Ormiston, another upholder of Wishart's ministry, was descended from the ancient House of Cockburn of that ilk, and was hereditary Constable of Haddington. One of Knox's earlier converts, he remained through life his attached and earnest friend. Chiefly on account of the support which he extended to Wishart he sustained severe persecution. By the Regent Arran and Archbishop Hamilton of St Andrews, he was, in 1548, forfeited and banished ; but he obtained his freedom by consenting to underlie the law. Knox, when detained in France, transmitted to his care Balnaves' "Treatise on Justification," which was found at Longniddry long afterwards.† In October 1559 he received at Berwick, from Sir Ralph Sadler and Sir James Crofts, £1000 sterling for the benefit of the poor who professed the Reformed faith : also, two hundred crowns (£63, 6s. 8d.) for his own use. Of the entire treasure he was deprived by the Earl of Bothwell and his retainers on his homeward journey. Cockburn's wife, Alison, daughter of Sir James Sandilands of Calder, was also a zealous supporter of the Reformed doctrines.

Under the protection of these three landowners, Wishart con-

* Acta Parl. Scot., vol. ii., p. 546.
† Three Scottish Reformers, Edin., 1874, p. 20.

ducted Divine service in the parish church of Inveresk, near Musselburgh, both in the morning and afternoon of the Sunday succeeding that on which he had preached at Leith. In connection with these services, Knox relates two incidents. As the people assembled for worship, two friars from the chapel of Loretto, at Musselburgh,* stood at the entrance of the church and whispered to those who entered. Remarking their procedure, Wishart invited them to enter. "Come in," he said, "and you shall hear the Word of Truth, which, according as you receive it, will prove to you a savour of life or of death." The friars still lingered at the door, and as the preacher denounced idolatrous worship, they again sought to divert the attention of those who stood near. Turning towards the scoffers, he exclaimed, "How long will you dare to deceive men's souls? You reject the truth yourselves, and would prevent others from embracing it. God will surely expose your hypocrisy and confound your malice."†

The other incident was of a more hopeful character. At the close of the afternoon's service, Sir George Douglas, brother of the Earl of Angus, stood up, and, in the hearing of the congregation, said, "I know that my Lord Governor and the cardinal will hear that I have been present at these services. I shall make no denial, and I will fearlessly defend the preacher and uphold his doctrines."‡

---

* Knox describes the loungers as two Grey Friars. The members of the chapel of Loretto were so designated, though not strictly entitled to the appellative. The chapel at Loretto, or Alareit, near Musselburgh, was founded in 1533, by Thomas Douchtie, and by him dedicated to the Virgin. Within the building, Douchtie and his successors professed to work miracles. In 1536, James V. made a pilgrimage to the chapel from Stirling, after being driven back by a storm on his first voyage to France to bring home his queen. A political pasquinade, at the expense of Douchtie and his brethren, the Grey Friars, was composed by Alexander Cunningham, fifth Earl of Glencairn. In this composition he names a Friar Laing, who, very probably, was one of those associated with the incident at Inveresk (Three Scottish Reformers, pp. 12-16).

† Knox's History, edit. 1846, vol. i., p. 135.

‡ Sir George Douglas of Pittendreich was an especial favourite of Henry VIII. In his society, when acting as one of the Scottish Commissioners, Wishart returned to Scotland. Appointed a Privy Councillor in March 1543, he was forfeited by the Catholic party for alleged treason, but was assoilzied in Decem-

As the governor and cardinal were now in Edinburgh, only a few miles distant, Wishart was, for greater safety, conducted to the mansion of Longniddry. There he had an opportunity of communing with Knox, who, deeply interested in his missionary labours, became his companion from place to place, armed with a two-handed sword.*

The mansion of Longniddry was situated in the parish of Gladsmuir, within four miles of the considerable village of Tranent. At Tranent Wishart preached to large assemblies on two consecutive Sundays. Attended by Knox, he proceeded to the town of Haddington on the 14th January 1545-6. There he was entertained by David Forrest, a respectable burgess who had embraced the Reformed doctrines. In dread of persecution, Forrest afterwards sought shelter in England.† He was, by the General Assembly of December 1560, nominated as one "apt and able to minister;" but though the request that he would enter the ministry was more than once renewed, he preferred to remain a layman. Latterly he was appointed General of the Mint. ‡

Wishart preached at Haddington two days in succession. Knox expected he would have large audiences, but was disappointed. At the first morning service a considerable number were present, but at the afternoon service, and the morning service of the second day, the attendance was "slender." The people, it was found, were unwilling to offend the Earl of Bothwell, who held lands in the neighbourhood, and was known to be in alliance with the cardinal. At the close of the first day's service, Wishart was entertained at the seat of Sir Richard Maitland of Lethington, father of William Maitland, the well-known statesman. Sir Richard was an industrious scholar, and without committing himself to the

---

ber 1544. He was constituted an Extraordinary Lord of Session in 1549. David, his eldest son, became seventh Earl of Angus; and his second son, James, was Earl of Morton and Regent of Scotland (Hay's Senators of the College of Justice, Edin., 1832, p. 94).

* Knox's History, edit. 1846, vol. i., p. 136.
† Sadler's Letters, vol. i., p. 585.
‡ Knox's Works, edit. 1846, vol. i., p. 563, note by Mr David Laing.

new opinions, was favourable to inquiry.* As on the second morning he was making preparations for service, Wishart received a letter from the Lords Cassilis and Glencairn, intimating that they were unable to meet him at Edinburgh. Apprehending that they had become indifferent to the Reformed cause, he was deeply moved, and remarked "that he was weary of the world since men were weary of God." Unable to afford him any substantial comfort, Knox begged that he would not disqualify himself for present duties.

After walking about half-an-hour before the high altar, Wishart ascended the pulpit. Perceiving that few were present, he said, "Lord, how long shall it be that Thy healing Word shall be despised, and men shall not regard their own salvation? I have heard of thee, O Haddington! that thou would'st send to the foolish Clerk Plays two or three thousand persons ; but of those in thy town and parish, not one hundred will assemble to hear the message of the eternal God." After some severe and pointed warnings, he proceeded with an exposition of the Second Table of the Law, and an exhortation to patience.† It had been arranged that Wishart should, in the evening, repair to Ormiston, the seat of his friend Cockburn. Before leaving Haddington he had a solemn parting with Douglas of Longniddry, and John Knox. As Knox expressed a desire to continue his attendant, he strictly forbade him. Relieving him of his two-handed sword, he said to him, "Return to your bairns,‡ and God bless you : one is sufficient for a sacrifice." The Reformers did not again meet. In his journey to Ormiston, Wishart was accompanied by John Cockburn, his host ; John Sandilands, younger of Calder,

---

* Sir Richard Maitland of Lethington held office under James V., Mary of Guise, Queen Mary, and James VI. He was knighted in 1551 on being appointed an Extraordinary Lord of Session. His "Collection of Early Scottish Poetry" is a work of great value. Poems of his own composition are printed by the Maitland Club. He died on the 20th March 1586 at the age of ninety.

† Knox's History, edit. 1846, vol. i., pp. 136-138.

‡ Children or pupils.

Cockburn's brother-in-law;* and Crichton of Brunstone.† Having reached Ormiston, the friends supped together; and thereafter Wishart discoursed respecting the death of God's chosen servants, concluding the evening's devotions by singing a metrical version of the 51st Psalm.‡ Wishing his friends refreshing rest, he retired to his apartment.

The Provincial Synod met at Edinburgh on the 13th January, but Beaton at once adjourned it till after Easter, promising to those assembled, that in the interval he would put to silence a heretic who was giving him much concern by disturbing the Church. Obtaining the co-operation of the Earl of Bothwell, as Sheriff of Haddingtonshire, he accompanied that nobleman to Elphinstone Tower at the head of five hundred men.§ The preacher's arrival at Ormiston being duly reported, Bothwell resolved to gratify the cardinal by effecting his capture. At midnight the house of Ormiston was surrounded by troops, while Cockburn and his guests were summoned to a surrender. To Cockburn, Bothwell volunteered the promise, that should Wishart be delivered into his hands, he would become personal surety for his safety, even against the power of the cardinal himself.

Informed that he was sought for, Wishart said meekly, " Let the will of the Lord be done." He addressed Bothwell in these words : "I thank God that one so honourable as your lordship receives me this night, being assured that, having

* John Sandilands was elder of the two sons of Sir James Sandilands of Calder. His younger brother was created Lord Torphichen. Knox resided in Calder House after his return to Scotland in 1555.

† Knox relates that on account of the keen frost, and the imperfect condition of the roads, the journey from Haddington to Ormiston was performed on foot. The distance was about six miles.

‡ Knox quotes the two opening lines :

" Have mercy on me now, good Lord,
    After thy great mercy," etc.

A paraphrase of the psalm commencing with these lines is contained in the " Gude and Godlie Ballates," edited or composed by John and Robert Wedderburn, who were living at Dundee about the year 1540.

§ Diurnal of Occurrents, p. 41.

pledged your honour, you will preserve me from injury without order of law. The law, I am not ignorant, is corrupt, and is used as a cloak under which to shed blood ; but I less fear to die openly than to be slain in secret." " Not only," replied Bothwell, " shall I protect you from secret violence, but I shall shelter you from the designs both of the governor and cardinal. In my keeping you shall be secure till I restore you to freedom or bring you again to this place." Accepting this engagement, Cockburn offered the earl his bond of manrent in token of service.

Bothwell bore Wishart to Elphinstone Tower. Having secured so important a prisoner, the cardinal despatched to Ormiston James Hamilton of Stonehouse, Captain of Edinburgh Castle, to arrest the persons of John Cockburn, John Sandilands, and Crichton of Brunstone. Cockburn and Sandilands invited Hamilton and his followers to refreshment, and in the interval Crichton contrived to escape. Of the prisoners of the night, Wishart was confined in Elphinstone Tower, and Cockburn and Sandilands were sent to Edinburgh Castle.*

Ormiston House, where Wishart was captured, and which he is believed to have visited in the course of his previous ministrations, is now a ruin. Of the structure, a gable wall and some vaults only remain. Adjoining the gable is a flower-garden, containing a venerable yew, under which Wishart is said to have preached. The yew is of a remarkable size, the stem extending to a girth of seventeen feet and reaching a height of thirty-three. Within the adjoining chapel a monumental brass commemorates Alexander, eldest son of John Cockburn, Wishart's host—a favourite pupil of Knox. A youth of high promise, he died in August 1564, at the age of twenty-nine. His epitaph, composed by Buchanan, proceeds thus :

" Omnia quæ longa indulget mortalibus ætas,
    Hæc tibi Alexander, prima juventa dedit,

---

* Knox's History, edit. 1846, vol. i., pp. 141, 142.

Cum genere et forma generoso sanguine digna ;
  Ingenium velox, ingenuumque animum.
Excoluit virtus animum, ingeniumque camenæ
  Successu studio consilioque pari ;
His ducibus primum peragrata Britannia deinde ;
  Gallia ad armiferos qua patet Helvetios ;
Doctus ibi linguas quas Roma, Sion, et Athenæ,
  Quas cum Germano Gallia docta sonat
Te licet in prima rapuerunt fata juventa :
  Non immaturo funere raptus obis,
Omnibus officiis vitæ qui functus obivit
  Non fas hunc vitæ est de brevitate queri.

> Hic conditur Mr Alexander Cockburn
> primogenitus Joannis domini Ormiston
> et Alisonæ Sandilands, ex preclara
> familia Calder, qui natus 13 Januarii 1535
> Post insignem linguarum professionem ;
> Obiit anno ætatis suæ 28 calen. Sept^t."

Sir John Cockburn, a younger brother of Knox's pupil, became a Lord of Session, and died in 1623. Other representatives of the family were distinguished as lawyers and statesmen. The barony of Ormiston now belongs to the Earl of Hopetoun.

From his confinement in Edinburgh Castle John Sandilands was liberated on granting the cardinal his bond of manrent.* Cockburn escaped by scaling the wall. In the Treasurer's book it appears that, on the 10th March 1546, John Paterson, pursuivant, received a fee of ten shillings for arresting " the gudes " of the Laird of Ormiston, and summoning him " to underly the law " at Edinburgh on the 13th April, " for resetting of Maister George Wishart, he being at the horne ;" also " for breking of the waird within the castell of Edinburgh."

As an important prisoner, Wishart was strictly guarded. Elphinstone Tower, his first prison, still remains a memorial alike of feudal dignity and ecclesiastical oppression. An oblong square keep, fifty-nine feet in length, it rises to a height of about eighty feet. The walls are from seven to twelve feet thick, and the several floors are supported on powerful arches. In the basement are the kitchen and servants' hall—

* Knox's History, edit. 1846, vol. i., p. 142.

the baron's hall occupies the second floor, and the third contains two large sleeping-apartments and other chambers. Passages are constructed within the walls, to which light is admitted by arrow-slit windows. This keep was reared in the thirteenth century by John de Elphinstone, who owned the adjoining lands. In Wishart's time it belonged to a descendant of Johnstone of that ilk. John Ker, minister of Prestonpans, and stepson of John Knox, married a daughter of John Johnstone of Elphinstone. After several changes the tower and lands were acquired by an ancestor of the present Baron Elphinstone. Wishart was immured in a narrow chamber on the basement floor. His first jailer, Patrick, Earl of Bothwell, was only less cruel, crafty, and unscrupulous than his more notorious son, the murderer of Darnley. Succeeding to the earldom in early life, he proved so obnoxious to public order, that James V., after twice subjecting him to imprisonment, deprived him of his lands in Liddesdale, and banished him from the kingdom. In England he engaged in treasonable negotiations with Henry VIII. Returning to Scotland on the death of James V., he attached himself to Beaton. Sir Ralph Sadler, in May 1543, describes him as "the most vain and insolent man in the world, full of pride and folly." * Imprisoned for disorderly practices, he was liberated, after the battle of Pinkie, in September 1547. He latterly obtained shelter at the court of Edward VI., and in 1556 closed in exile a life of shame.

Bothwell's promise to protect his prisoner from the vengeance of his adversaries was soon exchanged for another of a very opposite character. Wishart was made prisoner on the 16th January,† and, on the 19th of the same month, Bothwell, at a meeting of the Privy Council, pledged himself to deliver his prisoner to the order of the governor. The proceedings of the council are recorded in these words : ‡

* Sadler's State Papers, vol. i., p. 184.
† Diurnal of Occurrents, p. 41.
‡ Reg. Sec. Conc., fol. 25.

"Apud Edinburgh presente domino gubernatore xix° Januarii
    anno Domini millesimo v° xlv^to. Sederunt Cardinalis can-
    cellarius, Episcopus Candide Case, Comes Bothuel—
    Abbates paslay culros, dominus Borthuik, Clericus Registri.
"The quhilk day in presens of my Lord Gouernour and Lordis
of Counsel, Comperit Patrik Erle bothuel—and hes bundin and
oblist him to deliuer Maister george Wischart to my Lord Gouernour
or ony vtheris in his behalff, quham he will depute to ressaue him
betuix this and the penult day of Januar instant inclusive, and sall
kepe surelie and ansuer for him in the meyntyme vnder all the hiest
pane and chairge that he may incur giff he falzies herintill."

Between his two promises Bothwell halted in a manner
befitting his unstable and treacherous character. He conveyed his prisoner to Edinburgh; then, as if unwilling to
violate his engagement, brought him back to Haddingtonshire, and placed him in his castle of Hailes.* There he
proposed to hold him fast, but the queen regent promised
to renew her favour, which had been withdrawn, and the cardinal offered money if he would place his prisoner in Edinburgh Castle. Bothwell at length complied.†

At Edinburgh Castle Wishart was kept a few days only.
With the governor's sanction, he was removed by the cardinal
to his castle of St Andrews, and there confined in the sea-
tower. This terrible memorial of priestly tyranny remains
entire. Situated at the north-west corner of the spacious
quadrangle, which was enclosed by the other buildings of the
stronghold, the walls of the sea-tower are of enormous thick-
ness. Within is an arched chamber, about thirteen feet
square. From the centre, pierced in the solid rock, a circular
vault descends to a depth of twenty-seven feet, the upper
diameter being seven, and the lower seventeen feet. In this
loathsome pit were confined those who dared to oppose the
canon law or resist the authority of the Church. Here John
Roger, a black friar, was immured before his secret murder

* Hailes Castle occupies a retired spot on the banks of the Tyne, in the parish
of Prestonkirk. It is now a ruin.
† Knox's History, ed. 1846, vol. i., p. 143.

in 1544; and here George Wishart languished four weeks. Closely identified with the preacher's last days, the castle of St Andrews claims further notice. Reared in 1200 by Roger, Bishop of St Andrews, as his episcopal residence, it frequently changed hands during the War of Independence. Within it James I. received from Bishop Wardlaw his early education, James II. took counsel with the ingenious Bishop Kennedy, and James III. is supposed to have been born. During the primacy of Cardinal Beaton the castle was fitted to endure a siege.

Though Wishart was a prisoner in his castle, the cardinal encountered some difficulties in effecting his death. Friar John Roger had been secretly removed from the dungeon, and thrust headlong from the rock.* But George Wishart, as the scion of an ancient house, and an associate of several of the nobility, might not be summarily disposed of. The Church might condemn, but a fatal sentence could only be carried out on the authority of the governor. To the governor Beaton applied, desiring him to appoint a commission, with a criminal judge, to conduct the business of the trial. Unwilling to offend his powerful rival, Arran would have granted this request, but for the vigorous remonstrance of Sir David Hamilton of Preston, who pointed to the cardinal's ambition, and the unwarrantable character of his demand. Arran, accordingly, refused the commission, and expressed his desire that in the meantime all proceedings should be stopped.†

The cardinal had to encounter another difficulty. Gavin Dunbar, Archbishop of Glasgow, he well knew, regarded him with dislike, consequent on an extraordinary quarrel which had occurred between them eight months before. The circumstances of this dispute are peculiarly illustrative of that spirit of intolerance in Scottish churchmen which, with other errors, George Wishart condemned in his prelections and by his example. The cardinal happened to be in Glasgow when,

* Knox's History, ed. 1846, vol. i., p. 119.
† Lindsay of Pitscottie's History of Scotland, Edin., 1727, folio, p. 188.

on the 4th June 1545, the Sieur Gabriel de Montgomery*
arrived from France with auxiliary troops. In honour of the
occasion a solemn procession was arranged in the cathedral
church. As cardinal, *legatus natus*, and primate, Beaton
asserted the right of precedence, while Dunbar argued that as
archbishop of the diocese he was entitled to the priority. The
quarrel was taken up by the cross-bearers of the rival prelates,
who, at the door of the choir, engaged in open conflict. Both
crosses were thrown down, and the vestments of the bel-
ligerents were torn and scattered. This quarrel between the
cardinal and the archbishop, was, according to Knox, "judged
mortal and without any hope of reconciliation."†

Had Archbishop Dunbar refused to attend the proposed
convention at St Andrews, the cardinal might have failed to
effect his purpose. He was, however, keenly desirous of
upholding the Church by the destruction of heretics, and
so, laying aside private feeling, he consented to take part in
the approaching trial.

By the cardinal the bishops were invited to meet in his
cathedral on the 28th of February. The day before, John
Winram, the sub-prior, visited the prisoner and summoned him
to his trial. "It is," said the preacher, "useless for the cardinal to summon one to attend his court who is wholly in his
power. But observe your forms."

On the morning of the trial the bishops were ushered into
the cathedral by the cardinal's retainers. An armed party
fetched the prisoner, who, on entering the gate of the cathedral, threw his purse to a beggar, remarking that it would no

---

* James Montgomery de Lorges succeeded, in 1545, John Stuart, Count
D'Aubigny, as captain of the Scottish guard in France. He died in 1560.
Gabriel, his eldest son, mentioned in the text, obtained a painful notoriety from
having mortally wounded in a tournament Henry II. of France, in June 1559.
He retired to Normandy, and afterwards visited Italy and England. Subsequent
to 1562 he acted as a commander of the Protestant party in the religious wars of
France. He narrowly escaped destruction at the Massacre of St Bartholomew,
and two years later, having invaded Normandy, he was taken prisoner, and
executed on the 27th May 1574.

† Diurnal of Occurrents, p. 39; Knox's History, ed. 1846, vol. i., pp. 145-147.

longer be useful to himself. A discourse preached by Winram opened the proceedings.

In selecting Winram to preach, Beaton acted with his usual policy. A churchman of considerable rank and known ability, Winram was suspected of tolerating the new opinions. By being called on publicly to denounce them, the cardinal imagined that, out of respect to his own consistency, he would feel bound to conform to the ancient doctrines. Winram probably suspected the snare, and so did not fall into it. Choosing as his subject the Parable of the Sower, he described the Word of God as the good seed, and characterised heresy as the evil seed. Heresy consisted, he said, of opinions obstinately maintained which impugned the authority of Scripture. It was manifested on the part of those who had the care of souls, by wilful ignorance or neglect of the pastoral duties. A spiritual teacher ought thoroughly to understand that Word which he professed to explain to others. In the words of St Paul, " a bishop must be blameless, as the minister of God, not stubborn, not soon angry, not given to wine, no fighter, not given to filthy lucre, but a dispenser of hospitality, a lover of good men, sober, just, holy, temperate, holding fast the word of doctrine, that he may be able to exhort with wholesome learning, and to convince the gainsayers."* As the goldsmith had a test for the true metal, so the test of heresy was Holy Scripture. Respecting the punishment of heresy in this life, he read in the parable, " Let both grow together until the harvest."† Nevertheless, persistent opposition to the truth might be punished by the secular arm.

This discourse might have been addressed to any Protestant assembly. It certainly did not commit the preacher to an approval of the cardinal's proceedings. At the Reformation in 1560, Winram joined the Protestant party, and became associated with Knox and others in preparing the Confession of Faith and the First Book of Discipline.

At the close of Winram's discourse, Wishart was invited to

* Titus i. 7. † Matt. xiii. 30.

ascend the pulpit, there to answer the articles of accusation. John Lauder,* a priest and member of the Priory, stood forward as accuser. Reading the articles of indictment with unbecoming haste,† he demanded of the prisoner an immediate answer. After on his knees engaging in solemn prayer, Wishart rose, and said, "Words abominable even to conceive have been ascribed to me, wherefore hear and know my doctrine: Since my return from England, I have taught the Ten Commandments, the Twelve Articles of Faith, and the Lord's Prayer. In Dundee I expounded St Paul's Epistle to the Romans; and the manner of my teaching I shall presently explain——"

"Renegade, traitor, and thief!" exclaimed Lauder, "you have been a preacher too long, and have exercised your function without authority."

The bishops having concurred, Wishart expressed a desire that he might be tried by the governor.

"The cardinal is a judge, more than sufficient for thee," said Lauder. "Is not my Lord Cardinal Chancellor of Scotland, Archbishop of St Andrews, Bishop of Mirepois, Commendator of Arbroath, *legatus natus*, and *legatus a latere?*"—"I do not depise my Lord Cardinal," rejoined the preacher, "but I desire to be tried by the requirements of Holy Scripture, under the authority of the governor, whose prisoner I am."

"Such man, such judge," exclaimed the bystanders, while the cardinal proposed to pronounce sentence.

On further consideration, it was ruled that, better to justify the proceedings, the charges should be read a second time, and the prisoner questioned upon each.

"Renegade, traitor, and thief," proceeded Lauder, "thou hast deceived the people, and despised Holy Church, and the authority of the governor. Prohibited from preaching in

---

* John Lauder studied at St Andrews. His name appears among the licentiates in Pedagogio, anno 1508. It appears from the Treasurer's Accounts that he was frequently employed in ecclesiastical affairs.

† That Lauder spit in the prisoner's face, as is stated by Knox, may not be credited. Such an indecency would not have been tolerated either by the bishops or the spectators (Knox's History, ed. 1846, vol. i., p. 152).

Dundee, thou didst continue. So when the Bishop of Brechin cursed thee, delivered thee to the devil, and commanded thee to cease preaching, thou didst obstinately disobey."—"I read in Holy Scripture," answered Wishart, "that we ought to obey God rather than man."

"False heretic, thou didst say that a priest at the altar saying mass was as a fox in summer wagging his tail."—"The external motion of the body," replied the preacher, "without grace in the heart, is like the play of a monkey. God searches the heart, and those who truly worship Him must worship Him in sincerity. Such is my teaching."

"Thou hast falsely taught that there are not seven sacraments," said Lauder.—"I believe," replied Wishart, "in those sacraments only which were instituted by Christ, and are set forth in the Holy Gospel."

"Thou hast denied the Sacrament of Confession, affirming that men ought to confess sin to God, and not to the priest." —"I teach, my lord," said Wishart, "that priestly confession has no warrant, but that confession to God is blessed. In the 51st Psalm David makes confession to God, saying, 'Against Thee, Thee only, have I sinned.' When St James writes, 'Confess your faults one to another,' * he counsels us against being high-minded, and so to acknowledge our sinfulness before all. This do not the Grey Friars, who say they are already pure."

The bishops expressed a strong dissent, while Lauder proceeded to read the fifth article:

"False heretic, thou didst affirm that it was essential that man should understand the nature of baptism."—"My lord," said Wishart, "none of you would transact business with one to whose language you were a stranger. So the parent should understand what in baptism he undertakes for his child."

"Thou hast the spirit of error!" exclaimed a chaplain of the cardinal. Lauder went on:

"False heretic, traitor, and thief, thou didst set forth that the sacrifice of the altar was but a piece of bread, and the

* James v. 16.

consecration of the Eucharist a rite of superstition."—" Sailing on the Rhine," replied the preacher, "I met a Jew, with whom I reasoned respecting his religion. 'Messias, when He cometh, will not abrogate the law as ye do,' said the Jew; 'we support our poor, ye allow your needy to perish; we forbid the worship of images, your churches are full of idols; and ye adore a piece of bread, saying it is your God.' This incident I have related in my public teaching."

"Read the next article," interrupted the cardinal.

"False heretic, thou didst affirm that extreme unction was not a sacrament."—"To extreme unction I referred not in my teaching," was the preacher's reply.

"False heretic, thou didst deny the efficacy of holy water, and impugned the cursing of Holy Church."—"I never estimated the strength of holy water," said Wishart; "and I cannot commend exorcism or cursing while such have no warrant in the Holy Scripture."

"False renegade," proceeded Lauder, "thou hast denied the power of the Pope, and maintained that every layman is a priest."—"On the authority of the Word," replied the prisoner, "I taught that believers are 'a holy priesthood,' * and that those ignorant of the Scriptures, whatever their rank or degree, cannot instruct others; without the key of knowledge, they cannot bind or loose."

The bishops smiled derisively, while Lauder proceeded with the indictment.

"False heretic, thou hast denied the freedom of the will, and taught that man can of himself neither do good nor evil." —" Not so," answered the prisoner. "I teach in the words of Holy Scripture: 'Whosoever committeth sin is the servant of sin;' and, 'If the Son shall make you free, ye shall be free indeed.'" †

"False heretic," said Lauder, reading the eleventh article, "thou hast said that it is lawful to eat flesh on Friday."—"In the writings of St Paul I read," replied Wishart, "'Unto the pure, all things are pure, but unto those that are defiled and

* 1 Peter ii.   † John viii. 34, 36.

unbelieving is nothing pure.'   Through the Word the faithful
man sanctifies God's creatures : the creature may not sanctify
that which is corrupt."

   " That is blasphemy," said the bishops.

   " Thou hast taught, false heretic," continued the accuser,
"that men should pray to God only, and not to the saints.
Answer, yea or nay." — " The first commandment," replied
Wishart, "teaches me to worship God only ; and, as St Paul
writes, there is only 'one mediator between God and men,
the man Christ Jesus.' *   He is the door by which we must
enter in.   He that entereth not by this door, but climbeth
up some other way, the same is a thief and a robber.†   Concerning the saints, we are not taught to pray to them, and it
is not certain that they will hear us."

   " False heretic, thou sayest there is no purgatory."—" In
the Scriptures," replied the preacher, "such a place is not
named."

   " Thou hast falsely contemned the prayers of monks and
friars, and taught that priests may marry, and have wives."
—" I read in St Matthew's Gospel," was the Reformer's reply,
" that those who abstain from marriage for the kingdom of
heaven's sake are blessed of God.‡   Those who have not the
gift of chastity, and yet have become celebates, ye know have
erred greatly."

   " Renegade and heretic, thou hast refused to obey our
general and provincial councils." — " Should your councils
teach according to the Word of God, I shall obey them," was
the answer.

   " Proceed with the articles," shouted John Scot of the Greyfriars' monastery.

   " Thou hast taught that God dwells not in churches built
by men's hands, and that it is vain to consecrate costly edifices
to His praise."—" God," replied Wishart, " is present everywhere.   ' Behold,' said Solomon, ' heaven and the heaven of
heavens cannot contain Thee : how much less this house
which I have built.'§   In the Book of Job God is described

   * 1 Tim. ii. 5.   † John x. 1.   ‡ Matt. xix. 12.   § 2 Chron. vi. 18.

as 'high as heaven: deeper than hell: His measure longer
than the earth, and broader than the sea.'* Yet God is
pleased to honour places specially dedicated to His worship:
'Where two or three,' said the Saviour, 'are gathered together in my name, there am I in the midst of them.'† God
is certainly present where He is truly worshipped."

"Thou hast, false heretic, averred that men ought not to
fast."—"Fasting," replied the prisoner, "is commended in
Scripture; and I have learned by experience that fasting is
beneficial to the body. God honoureth those only who truly
fast."

"False heretic, thou hast said that the souls of men do
sleep until the Day of Judgment."—"God forgive those who
so report me," replied Wishart. "The soul of the believer
does not sleep, but at once enters into glory."

As the preacher closed, the bishops returned a verdict of
"guilty." Wishart, on his knees, expressed these words of
prayer: "Gracious and everlasting God, how long wilt Thou
permit Thy servants to suffer through infatuation and ignorance? We know that the righteous must suffer persecution
in this life, which passeth as doth a shadow, yet we would
entreat Thee, merciful Father, that Thou wouldest defend Thy
people whom Thou hast chosen, and give them grace to
endure and continue in Thy Holy Word."

Having commanded the laity to retire, the cardinal sen-
tenced the prisoner to be burned to ashes. By the captain
of the castle and his warders, Wishart was conducted to his
prison. There he was visited by two monks from the Greyfriars' monastery, John Scot and another, who offered to act
as his confessors. He declined their offer, but expressed a
desire that the sub-prior might be sent to him. Winram
joined him at once; but the subject of their conversation did
not transpire.

The execution was fixed for the 1st of March, the day after
the trial. A stake was erected in the centre of an open
space fronting the principal entrance to the castle. The

main tower, the several turrets, and front windows were
decorated with silk hangings and tapestry ; and the prisoner's
escape was rendered impossible by the heavy artillery of the
fortress being pointed towards the scene of execution.

From the front windows of the castle, the cardinal and
bishops reclined on splendid cushions. The cardinal's military
guard, bearing insignia, encircled the stake. As the trum-
peters sounded, two executioners proceeded to fetch the
prisoner. They arrayed him in a vestment of black linen,
and hung bags of gunpowder around his person ; then they
conducted him to the place of death.

" Pray to our Lady, Master George," exclaimed two friars,
as the prisoner crossed the drawbridge.   " Tempt me not, my
brethren," replied the preacher.

At the stake, Wishart fell upon his knees, and exclaimed
aloud : "Saviour of the world, have mercy upon me.
Heavenly Father, into Thy hands I commend my spirit."
Turning to the multitude, he said : "Christian brethren and
sisters, be not offended at the Word of God on account of the
tortures you see prepared for me.   Love the Word which
publisheth salvation, and suffer patiently for the Gospel's sake.
To my brethren and sisters who have heard me elsewhere,

declare that my doctrine is no old wife's fables, but the
blessed Gospel of salvation. For preaching that Gospel, I am
now to suffer, and I suffer gladly for the Redeemer's sake.
Should any of you be called on to endure persecution, fear
not them who can destroy the body, for they cannot slay the
soul. Most falsely have I been accused of teaching that the
soul shall sleep after death till the last day; I believe my
soul shall sup with my Saviour this night." After a pause,
he said, "I beseech you, brethren and sisters, exhort your
prelates to acquaint themselves with the Word of God, so
that they may be ashamed to do evil and learn to do good;
for if they will not turn from their sinful way, the wrath of
God shall fall upon them suddenly, and they shall not escape."
Again falling on his knees, he prayed for those who had,
through ignorance, condemned him, and for all who had
testified against him falsely. One of the executioners, who
entreated his forgiveness, he kissed on the cheek, saying to
him, " By this token I forgive thee ; do thine office." Wishart
was now made fast to the stake, while a heap of faggots
was piled around his body. Fire being applied, the bags of
gunpowder attached to his person exploded, and he ceased to
live.

Deeply moved, the multitude retired from the scene of
death. A religion which required such sacrifices could not
long retain general acceptance. But the cardinal was indifferent to public sentiment. Early in April he, at Finhaven in Forfarshire, attended the marriage of his illegitimate
daughter, Margaret, with David Lindsay, afterwards Earl of
Crawford. One of the charges on which Wishart was condemned, was that he opposed the celibacy of the clergy. But
while the cardinal held those who opposed priestly celibacy
to be worthy of death, he personally ignored its obligations.
For many years he cohabited with Marion Ogilvy, a daughter
of Lord Ogilvy of Airlie, by whom he was father of two sons
and a daughter, Margaret.* In a contract of marriage which
he subscribed at St Andrews on the 10th April 1546, he

* Knox's History, ed. 1846, p. 174, note by Mr David Laing.

names Margaret Beaton as his daughter, and as such he provided her with a dowry of four thousand merks.*

The account we have presented of Wishart's trial and martyrdom is derived from the narrative of Foxe the martyrologist, in the first edition of his "Actes and Monumentes," printed in 1563. The original of that narrative is contained in a black-letter volume,† printed at London by John Day and William Seres, with the title, "The tragical death of David Beatō, Bishoppe of Sainct Andrewes in Scotland, whereunto is ioyned the martyrdom of maister George Wyscharte, gentleman, for whose sake the aforesayed bishoppe was not long after slayne. Wherein thou maiest learne what a burnynge charitie they shewed not only towardes him : but vnto suche as come to their hādes for the blessed Gospel's sake." The volume is without a date, but the "Tragedy of Beaton" contained in it was composed by Sir David Lindsay about a year after the cardinal's death, and it is not improbable that the account of Wishart, by which it is accompanied, was prepared by Knox when he resided in the Castle of St Andrews, between April and July 1547. Whether this opinion be well founded or not, Knox has, by including in his "History" the narrative of the martyr's trial and death contained in the black-letter volume, substantially verified its details.

In the reprint of Foxe's "Actes and Monumentes," which appeared in 1570, on the margin opposite to Wishart's allusion to the bishops, are these words : "M. George Wishart prophesieth of the death of the cardinall, which followed after." Proceeding on this unwarrantable deduction, George Buchanan, in his "History of Scotland," asserts that, at the stake, Wishart did actually predict the cardinal's death. Adopting his uncle's statement, David Buchanan, in his edition of Knox's "History," ‡ adds that Wishart at the stake, "looking towards the cardinal, said, he who in such state

---

* Lord Lindsay's Lives of the Lindsays, London, 1858, 8vo, vol. i., p. 201.
† A unique copy of this volume belonged to the late Mr Richard Heber.
‡ Knox's History, edited by David Buchanan, Lond., 1644, p. 171.

D

from that high place feedeth his eyes with my torments, within few dayes shall be hanged out at the same window, to be seen with as much ignominy, as he now leaneth there in pride."

Other erroneous statements in connection with Wishart's execution may be related, since they have unhappily been adopted by more than one historian, and are generally believed. Lindsay of Pitscottie, an extremely credulous writer, remarks* "that Wishart informed the captain of the castle that he saw a great fire upon the sea, which, moving to and fro, at length came upon the city of St Andrews, and lighting upon the earth, brake asunder, which, he thought, did portend the wrath of God to seize shortly not only on that wicked man, who was lord of that castle, but also upon the city." George Buchanan† relates that the sub-prior, on being admitted to Wishart's presence, asked him whether he would receive the Holy Communion, when he answered that he would, provided it was dispensed in both the elements. Having communicated to the cardinal the prisoner's wish, Winram was censured for conveying it, while the request was denied. Next morning, at nine o'clock, the governor of the castle, on sitting down to breakfast, asked Wishart to eat with him. Wishart consented, and, with the governor's consent, consecrated bread and wine, and distributed to those who sat with him, also partaking himself. He then closed with prayer. This narrative has been incorporated by David Buchanan in his edition of Knox's "History."

Lindsay of Pitscottie's narrative betrays the credulous character of its author, and may be dismissed summarily. The statements of Buchanan are unsupported by Knox. As Knox was associated with Winram in preparing the standards of the Reformed Church, he was as likely as any other to obtain from him what he might divulge respecting his last interview with Wishart. But Knox remarks

* Lindsay of Pitscottie's History of Scotland, from 1431 to 1565, Edin., 1728, folio, p. 190.

† History of Scotland, by George Buchanan, Lond., 1690, folio, vol. ii., p. 96.

emphatically that " he could not show" what had occurred on that occasion.* Further, at the time that Wishart was at St Andrews undergoing his sufferings, Knox was resident in the neighbouring county of Haddington, while Buchanan was in exile. Knox, too, was an inmate of the castle in which the martyr was imprisoned, little more than a year after his death, and Buchanan did not compose his " History" till nearly thirty years afterwards. If the governor of the castle related that Wishart dispensed the Holy Communion, Knox must have heard the narrative, and he could have no motive for suppressing it. But it is extremely improbable that one occupying the position of governor of the cardinal's castle, would venture to allow a condemned heretic to consecrate the eucharist. By so doing, and more especially by partaking of the elements himself, he would have rendered himself liable to a charge of sacrilege, attended with imprisonment or death. Wishart, after his trial, would no doubt be carried back to his dungeon under the rude guardianship of unfeeling warders.

Wishart's alleged prediction as to Beaton's death is unnoticed in the black-letter volume printed shortly after his execution. Foxe, in his first and in the text of his subsequent editions, omits reference to it; and Knox, who ascribes to the martyr what he did not claim, a sort of foreknowledge, is silent on the point. But on other grounds the preacher has been charged with conspiring against the cardinal's life. And this charge must be fully met.

Wishart returned to Scotland at the close of July 1543, and in April of the following year, a person, described as a " Scottish man called Wyshert," bore from Crichton of Brunstone to the court of Henry VIII. a letter, of which the contents indicate a conspiracy for the destruction of the cardinal. The question arises as to whether the preacher and the messenger were one and the same person. To arrive at a proper conclusion, the conspiracy against Beaton must be considered in its details.

* Knox's History, Edin., 1846, vol. i., p. 168.

When James V. died unexpectedly in December 1542, there was found in his possession a roll, containing the names of three hundred and sixty persons suspected of heresy. The roll was in the handwriting of Beaton, who had desired the king to confiscate all who were named in it. To carry out his plans, Beaton presented a document, which he described as the king's will, constituting him governor of the kingdom, and guardian of the infant princess. That document was pronounced a forgery, and, by general consent, the Earl of Arran was appointed governor.*

A proposal for the marriage of the infant queen with the Prince of Wales was, in the interests of the Church, keenly opposed by the cardinal. Letters from him to the House of Guise, inviting armed resistance, being discovered, he was seized by the governor, and, on the charge of treason, warded in Blackness Castle. He regained his liberty, but in the meantime efforts were put forth by Henry VIII. to have him brought as a prisoner to England.† From among those whose lands the cardinal had proposed to confiscate, Henry found no difficulty in procuring the services of some well suited to his purpose. With these were joined a former friend of the cardinal, Alexander Crichton of Brunstone, a person of uncommon skill and vigorous enterprise. On Crichton's promise of co-operation, Henry honoured him with a private letter. Crichton acknowledged the royal missive, in a communication dated 16th November 1543, in which he assured Sir Ralph Sadler he would do his best to fulfil the king's wishes.‡

But the cardinal, though widely obnoxious, could not be assailed without much risk and difficulty. As chancellor of the kingdom, and a prince of the Church, any injury done to him would be adjudged treason. From many of the nobles and the principal landowners he had obtained bonds of manrent, by which they had become bound to support him with

* Sadler's State Papers, vol. i., pp. 94, 138.
† Ib., vol. i., pp. 221, 249, 278, 312.
‡ Ib., vol. i., p. 332.

their persons and goods.* Crichton therefore could not readily fulfil the wishes of his royal correspondent. The mission which he undertook in November 1543 was not in shape until the following April. Of the condition of affairs at that period, we are informed in the following communication from the Earl of Hertford to the king:

"Please it your Highnes to understande that this daye arryved here with me, the Erll of Hertforde, a Scottish man called Wyshert, and brought me a letter from the Larde of Brunstone, which I sende your Highnes herewith. And according to his request have taken order for the repayre of the said Wyshert to Your Majestie by poste, both for the delyvere of such letters as he hathe to Your Majestie from the saide Brunstone; and also for the declaracion of his credence whiche as I can perceyve by him consisteth in two poyntes: one is that the Larde of Graunge, late thresourer of Scotlande, the Mr. of Rothes, th' Erle of Rothes' eldest son, & John Charters wolde attempt eyther t' apprehend or slee the Cardynall at some tyme when he shall passe thoroughe the Fyflande, as he doth sundrye tymes to Sanct Andrewes: and in case they can so apprehend hym, will delyver him unto Your Majestie: which attemptat he saythe they wolde enterpryse if they knew Your Majesties pleasure therein: and what supportacion and mayntenance Your Majestie wolde mynister unto them efter th' execution of the same, in case they suld be per-sewed afterwards be any of theyr enemyes: the other is that in case your Maj: wolde grant unto them a conveniant enterteyne-ment for to kepe 1000 or 1500 men in wages for a moneth or two, they, joyning with the power of th' Erll Marshall, the saide Mr. of Rothes, the Larde of Calder, and others of the Lorde Grey's friends will tak upon them at such tyme as Your Maj: armye sall be in Scotland to destroye the abbey and towne of Arbroyth being the Cardynalles, and all th' other bisshopes and abbotes houses and countreys on that syde the water thereaboute; and t' appre-hende all those whiche they say be the principall impugnators of th' amyte betwen Englande and Scotlande: for the whiche they sulde have a good opportunytie, as they saye, when the power of the said bisshopes and abbotes sall resorte toward Edinburgh to resiste Your Majestyes armye. And for th' execution of these thinges the said

* Knox's History, edit. 1846, vol. i., p. 172.

Wyshert sayeth that the saide Erll Marshall and others above named will capitulate with your Majestie in wryting under their handes and seales afore they shall desyre any supplie or ayde of money at Your Majesties' handes. This is th' effect of his credence with other sondry advertisementes of the grit contencion and division that is at this present within the realme of Scotlande, whiche we doubt not he woll declair unto Your Majestie at good length.—Also I, the said Erll of Hertford, have recevyed this daye certene letters from the Lord Wharton and Sir Robert Bowes, with the copies of suche letters as were wrytten be the Erll of Glencarne's sone, & Bishop the Erll of Lennox's secretary, to be sent into Scotlande to the same Erlles : whiche copies the said Lord Wharton & Mr Bowes atteyned to suche meanes as sall appear unto your Majestie by theyr saide letters, whiche with the saide copies we send also to Your Highnes, here inclosed : together with certen other letters which arryved here also this day from the Lord Ewers, conteyning certen exploytes done in Scotlande. Fynally, the Lorde Wylyam Howard being at Tynemont sent a letter this morning to me, the said Erll of Hertford, whereby it appereth that certaine of the shippes victuallers are arryved there, and some of theym report that yesterday in the morning they sawe my Lord Admyrall with the reste of the fleete on see borde Hull makyng hitherwarde : so that the wynde contynuing as it is, they wilbe at Tynemont this night or to morrawe with the grace of God : who preserve Your Royall Majestie." *

This letter is endorsed, " Despeched xvij° Aprel at iiij°° at aft none."

In the preceding communication, Lord Hertford informs the king, through the messenger Wishart, that Crichton of Brunstone had made two propositions. In the first instance he undertook, on certain conditions, that the Master of Rothes, Kirkaldy of Grange, and Charteris of Kinfauns, would seize the cardinal, and either slay him or send him a prisoner into England. Or on obtaining from the English king the necessary support, the Earl Marischal, the Earl of Rothes, Sandilands of Calder, and other associates of Lord Gray, would destroy the Abbey of Arbroath, of which the cardinal was commendator, and from which he derived a por-

* State Papers, Henry VIII., vol. v., pp. 377, 378.

tion of his wealth. On the subject of these proposals, the
messenger, Wishart, was admitted by Henry to a private
interview, of which the result is set forth in the following
despatch from the Lords of the Privy Council to Lord Hertford :

"After our moost harty commendations unto your good Lordship.
These shalbe to signifye unto you that this bearer Wishert, which
cam from Brounston, hath bene with the King's Majestie, and for his
credence declared ever the same matiers in substance whereof
Your Lordship hath written hither : and hath received for answer
touching the Feats against the Cardinall, That in cace the Lords and
Gentlemen which he named shall enterprise the same ernestly and do
the best they can to th' uttermost of their powers to bringe the same
to passe indede ; and theruppon not being able to contynue longer in
Scotlande sholbe enforced to flye into this Realme for refuge, his
Highnes wilbe contented to accepte them & relief them as shall
appertyn. And as to their second desyre to have th' entretaynement
of a certayn nombre of men at his Highnes chargs, promisyng
therefore to covenaunt with His Majestie in writing under their seales
to burn and destroy the Abbots, Bishops, and other Kirkmen's lands,
His Majestie hath aunswered that forasmuch his Highnes Armey shall
be by the grace of God entred into Scotlande and redy to return
agayn before His Highnes can sende doun to them, and they sende
agayn and have aunswer for a conclusion in this matier, his Highnes
thinks the tyme too shorte to commune any further in it after this
sorte : But if they mynde effectually to him, and destroy as they have
offred at his Majestie's Armey being in Scotland ; and for their true
and upright dealyngs with His Majestie therin, will lay in to Your
Lordshipp, my Lord Lieutenant, such hostages as you shall think
convenient : his Highnes will take order that you my Lord, shall
delivre unto them one thousand punds sterling for their furnytures
in that behalf which his Majestie's pleasure is you shall cause to be
payed unto them in case they shall break with you in this matier ;
and delivre you such hostages as aforesayd. Thus fayre your Lordshipp right hartily well. From Grenewich the 26th of April 1544.

"Your good Lordship's assured loveing ∫frends Cherles Suffolk,
Tho. Weston, Ste. Winton, John Gage, T. Chene, Antony Wyng-
field, William Pagot." *

* Haynes' Collection of State Papers, Lond., 1740, folio, p. 32.

Here we arrive at a point whence to determine whether the messenger who conveyed to the Court of Henry VIII. Crichton's proposals for the destruction of the cardinal, was identical with the Reformed preacher.   The conspiracy, it will be remarked, had hitherto proceeded solely on political grounds. Henry desired the cardinal's destruction on account of his persistent opposition to the proposed alliance on which he had set his heart ; while Crichton sought to avenge a private feud, and his coadjutors to resent a scheme of confiscation.   Was Wishart the preacher likely to implicate himself in such a plot ?   Politically it was not for the interests of the Protestant cause that he should.   Could he have done so unknown to the cardinal, who, among the numerous charges brought against him at his trial, does not include that of treason or sacrilege ? Does Wishart's character, concerning which testimony is borne by two persons to whom he was personally known, warrant the belief that he would seek to destroy life ?   By Tylney he is described as " a man, modest, temperate, fearing God, hating covetousness, forgiving those who would have slain him, and seeking to do good to all and hurt to none."   Knox * styles him " a meek lamb," and further describes him as " a man of such graces, as before him were never heard within this nation."

Both in Lord Hertford's despatch to Henry VIII., and in the Privy Council's answer, Crichton's messenger is styled *Wyshert* or *Wishert.*   George Wishart was in holy orders, and was a Master of Arts.   His ecclesiastical connection is referred to in the letters contained in the Cottonian MSS.   He is described as a " clerk " by his contemporary Bishop Lesley,† who belonged to the Romish Church.   He is named as Master of Arts by Tylney, who remarks that he was " commonly called

---

* Knox's History, vol. i., pp. 125, 168.

† The History of Scotland, written in the Scottish vernacular for the use of Queen Mary, by John Lesley, Bishop of Ross.   Published by the Bannatyne Club in 1830, from a MS. belonging to the Earl of Leven, p. 191.   Bishop Lesley was born in 1526, and was therefore in his twentieth year at the period of Wishart's martyrdom.

Maister George of Bennet's College." He is styled "Maister George" by Knox.* In the Treasurer's Accounts† he also receives the prenomen of Master. Had Crichton been privileged to employ a messenger who was a Master of Arts and in orders, he would not have allowed the facts to remain unnoticed. And if his messenger had been the Cambridge scholar, whom the Scottish Commissioners took under their protection, it is absolutely certain that he would have said so. By the Earl of Hertford the messenger would have been described otherwise than as "a Scottish man called Wyshert."

But it may, we think, conclusively be shown who the messenger really was. There was a connection by marriage between the House of Wishart of Pitarrow and that of Learmont of Balcomie.‡ James Learmont of Balcomie was one of the commissioners employed in negotiating the marriage of the Prince of Wales with the infant Queen Mary. He was an avowed enemy of the cardinal, who latterly sought his apprehension.§ He was also an associate of Norman Leslie, to whose sister his son George was afterwards married.‖

At this period the members of the House of Pitarrow consisted of John Wishart, who owned the estate, his brother George the preacher, and James of "Carnebeg," his second brother, who was father of four sons, John, James, Alexander, and George. John Wishart, eldest son of James of Carnebeg, ultimately became a judge in the Supreme Court, and probably had a legal training. If he studied law at Edinburgh, he would in that city have an opportunity of meeting the associates of his kinsman, the Laird of Balcomie. Two of these associates, Norman Leslie, and Kirkaldy, younger of Grange, were early conspirators against the cardinal.

If John Wishart became Crichton's messenger, his designation in the Earl of Hertford's letter was sufficiently appropriate. His father, as a younger brother of the Laird of Pitarrow, owned only a small holding on the estate, and he

---

* Knox's History, ed. 1846, vol. i., pp. 125-169.
† Treasurer's Accounts, March 1546.
‡ See *supra*.　　　§ See *postea*.　　　‖ Douglas's Peerage, p. 588.

had himself no certain prospects, or any well-defined social status.

Was this John Wishart likely to support the cause of the Reformation by joining in a conspiracy against the cardinal? His career is depicted in the accompanying history of his House. He was an active promoter of the Protestant doctrines, and one of those who sat in Parliament when the Reformed Church was recognised. He was an adherent of the Regent Murray, who granted him land and honoured him with knighthood. But, like his contemporaries, Kirkaldy of Grange, and Maitland of Lethington, he lacked consistency. As paymaster of the Reformed clergy, his conduct was doubtful. He deserted the Regent Murray, who was largely his benefactor. He joined Kirkaldy of Grange when he held the Castle of Edinburgh on behalf of the dethroned queen, and in virtual opposition to the Protestant government. He rejoiced in contention, and was chargeable with avarice. Having joined Kirkaldy on behalf of Queen Mary, in 1573, he was not unlikely to have associated with the same wavering statesman in plotting the death of Beaton about thirty years previously.

But George Wishart the preacher was, on the father's side, uncle of John Wishart, the supposed conspirator. If the preacher was cognisant that his nephew joined in the conspiracy, he was personally identified with it. Doubtless so. But there is no evidence that he was informed of it. He seems to have resided at Pitarrow from the period of his return to Scotland, in July 1543, till the spring of 1545, when he commenced preaching at Montrose. The "Scottish man called Wyshert" appears in connection with the conspiracy only in April 1544. If, as we conjecture, John Wishart was studying law at Edinburgh when Learmont of Balcomie made him known to the cardinal's enemies, he may have proceeded on his expedition to the English court without communicating with his relatives at Pitarrow. On the messenger's return, the plot slumbered, and it was not revived till the following spring, when the name of Wishart no longer appears in the list of conspirators. Is it an unwarrantable hypothesis that, being latterly informed of his doings, his uncle, the preacher, persuaded him to withdraw from the conspiracy?

Till George Wishart's death, the conspirators made no definite arrangements. They were now actuated by a deadly revenge, which was probably stimulated by Learmont of Balcomie, the martyr's relative. It would appear the final plot was in active progress a few weeks after the martyrdom, for, on his return from Finhaven early in April, the cardinal learned that he was in danger. Attending the Provincial Synod at Edinburgh, in the end of April, the Earl of Angus made an attempt to destroy him.* On his return to St Andrews, he gave instructions that the castle should be repaired and fortified. He next summoned the landowners of Fife to meet him at Falkland, on Monday the 31st May, ostensibly to consider public affairs, but with the actual purpose of apprehending those persons whose enmity he most dreaded, among whom were Norman Leslie, John Leslie, his uncle, Kirkaldy of Grange, and Learmont of Balcomie.

His purpose was anticipated. On the evening of Friday the 28th of May, Norman Leslie, with several followers, entered St Andrews, and proceeded to his usual inn. Kirkaldy, younger of Grange, had arrived previously; and John Leslie, whose hostility to the cardinal was well known, came during the night. Next morning the conspirators and their followers, numbering sixteen persons, walked in detached groups in the grounds of the cathedral. On a signal that the drawbridge was lowered to admit the workmen, Norman Leslie with his followers entered the castle. Engaging the porter in conversation, he enabled James Melville of Raith and William Kirkaldy to cross the drawbridge unobserved. When John Leslie came up, the porter attempted to secure the portcullis, but was struck down. Finding the castle in possession of an armed band, the workmen threw down their tools and dispersed. Kirkaldy guarded a private postern, while his associates aroused the servants and conducted them

* Knox's History, ed. 1846, vol. i., p. 172.

from the stronghold. Hearing the noise, the cardinal threw
open his window and inquired the cause. Informed that
Norman Leslie had taken the castle, he attempted to escape
by the postern. Finding that it was guarded, he returned
to his chamber, and piled the heavier furniture against the
door. John Leslie knocked loudly, and, announcing his
name, demanded admission. "I will have Norman," said the
cardinal, "for he is my friend." "Be content with such as
are here," was the rejoinder; and on a call for fire, the
cardinal opened. John Leslie and another rushed upon him
with their swords, but James Melville entreated them to
pause, and adjured the cardinal to prepare for death. He
especially exhorted him to repent of the murder of Wishart,
for which the Divine vengeance had now overtaken him.
The conspirators then fell upon him with their swords. His
last words were, "Fy, fy, I am a priest, all is gone."[*]

The events of the morning were a terrible sequel to the
auto-da-fe of March. The citizens were in consternation.
The provost convened the town council, and, proceeding to
the ramparts of the castle, inquired whether the cardinal was
alive.[†] The answer was that he was dead, and, in hideous
evidence of the fact, his dead body was suspended on the
wall. Not long afterwards was formed, within the castle, the
first congregation of the Protestant Church in Scotland.

Though neither the first nor last of those who suffered,
George Wishart rendered to the cause of the Reformation in
Scotland real and important service. Through his instru-
mentality John Knox was led to exchange the retired life of
a private tutor for that of a public teacher of the Protestant
doctrines. Though his ministry was of short duration, he
lived at a time when men, who resisted prevailing error,
accomplished, within a few months, the work of a generation.
In Dundee his fervent preaching was long gratefully remembered. The singular devotedness of the Covenanters

---

[*] Knox's History, ed. 1846, vol. i., pp. 173-177.
[†] *Ib.*, vol. i., p. 178; Bishop Lesley's History of Scotland, Edin., 1830, 4to,
p. 19.

of Ayrshire was not more derived from the early confession
of the Lollards of Kyle,* than from the example and preaching
of George Wishart.

Wishart's character is celebrated by John Johnstone, in the
following epigram :

> " Quam bene conveniunt divinis nomina rebus
>   Divinæ hic Sophiæ corque oculusque viget
> Qui Patris arcanam Sophiam, cœlique recessus,
>   Corde fovens terris Numina tanta aperit
> Unus amor Christus.   Pro Christo concitus ardor
>   Altius humanis Enthea corda rapit,
> Præteritis aptans præsentia judicat omnia
>   Et ventura dehinc ordine quæque docet
> Ipse suam mortem tempusque modumque profatur
>   Fataque carnifici tristia sacrilego
> Terrificam ad flammam stat imperterritus.   Ipsa
>   Quin stupet invictos sic pavefacto animos
> Ut vix ausa dehinc sit paucos carpere.   Tota
>   Ilicet innocui victa cruore viri est."†

Describing Wishart as in the pulpit alike uncompromising
in the exposure of error as in reproving those who rejected
the Gospel message, Knox expatiates on the gentleness of
his private life. Tylney, who was his pupil at Cambridge,

* Calderwood's History of the Church of Scotland, vol. i., p. 49.
† MS. Poems of John Johnstone, in the Advocates Library, Edinburgh.   A
portion of the epigram has thus been rendered by an ingenious friend :

> " How good a thing it is in one to find,
> His name the mirror of a virtuous mind ;
> And well may Wishart claim the spotless heart
> Where heavenly wisdom breathes in every part ;
> Christ his sole love, he doth unfold the store,
> Of all his bosom holds of sacred lore.
> Celestial themes are his, and he displays
> The hidden mystery of the Father's ways ;
> Fired with the love of Christ, his zealous heart
> Prophetic soars above all human art.
>
> .   .   .   .   .
>
> Dauntless amidst devouring flames he stands,
> Which shrink as loath to kiss the martyr's hands ;
> No trembling victim now attests their rage,
> For fiercest fires doth innocence assuage."

remarks that he was "courteous" and "lowly." To the poor
at Cambridge he supplied food and raiment, and provided
some with monthly, and others with weekly donatives. A
diligent instructor, he assisted his pupils at their private read-
ings, as well as in the public school. Though of grave deportment, his manners were mild, rather than austere. He was
of a tall, slight figure, had a dark complexion, and wore a long
beard, and a small French cap. He dressed in "a fustian
doublet," with black stockings, and a frieze gown.

To his erudition and accomplishments Knox and Tylney
bear strong testimony. The bishops at St Andrews, who condemned him, did not venture to rebut his arguments. The
clergy at Bristol attempted his discomfiture only by violence.
Apart from the power of his public teaching, and the excel-
lence of his private virtues, he, as a martyr, holds a place on
the roll of the illustrious. He died to assert his testimony
against sacerdotal arrogance and priestly corruption, which are
the curse of nations. In his blood the Scottish Church took
root, and so long as his countrymen cherish Protestantism
and love liberty, his memory will be fragrant.

THE CONFESSION OF FAITH OF THE CHURCHES OF SWITZERLAND.

THE following English translation of the first Helvetian Confession was composed by George Wishart. The original Confession was under the direction of a conference held at Basel in January 1536, prepared in Latin by the Reformers Bullinger, Myconius, Grynaeus, Leo Juda, and Grossmann. In the following March it received the united sanction of the representatives of the different Swiss churches at a second conference at Basel. In versions of Latin and German it was submitted to an assembly at Wittenberg by Bucer and Capito, and also to the Protestant princes at the meeting at Smalkald in February 1537, and was on both occasions approved. Subsequent to the latter event, Wishart produced his English translation. From a unique copy, formerly in the possession of Mr Richard Heber, Wishart's version has been reprinted in the "Miscellany of the Wodrow Society." From that work it is transferred to these pages. The original is a tract of fifteen leaves octavo, in black letter. There is no date or printer's name, but it is believed to have been printed at London by Thomas Raynalde about the year 1548. The title-page is inscribed :

"This confescione was fyrste wrytten and set out by the ministers of the churche and congregacion of Sweuerland, where all godlynes is receyued, and the worde hadde in most reuerence, and from thence was sent unto the Emperour's maiestie, then holdynge a gryat counsell or parliamēt in the yeare of our Lord God, Md cxxxvii in the moneth of February. Translated out of laten by George Usher a Scotchman, who was burned in Scotland, the yeare of our lorde Mv c xlvi.

"OF THE HOLY SCRYPTURE.

"The Canonycall or holy Scrypture, whiche is the Worde of God, taught and gyven by the Holy Spryte, and publyshed unto the worlde by the prophetes and holy apostles, which also is the moost perfyte and auncient science and doctryne of wysdome, it alone contayneth consumatly all godlynes and all sorte and maner of facyon of lyfe.

"OF THE EXPOSICION OF SCRYPTURE.

"The interpretacion, or exposicion of this holy wrytte, ought and shuld be sought out of it selfe, so that it shulde be the owne interpretour, the rule of charite and faythe hauynge gouernaunce.

"OF MANNES TRADICIONS.

"As to other thyngs, of Tradicions of men, howe bewtifull and how moch receyued soeuer they be, what so euer tradicions withdraweth us and stoppeth us fro the Scripture, of such do we answere the sayinges of the Lorde, as of thyngs hurtfull and unprofytable, 'They worshippe me in vayne, teachying the doctrynes of man.' Mathi. 15.

"OF THE HOLY FATHERS.

"For the whiche sorte of interpretacyon so farre as the Holy Fathers hathe not gone fro it, not onely do we receyue them as interpretones of the Scripture, but also we honour and worshyp them as chosen and beloued instrumentes of God.

"THE ENDE AND ENTENTE OF THE SCRYPTURE.

"The pryncypal entent of al the Scripture canonicall is, to declare that God is beniuolent and frendly mynded to mankynde; and that he hathe declared that kyndnes in and throughe Jesu Chryste his onely sone: the which kyndnes is receyuyd by fayth; but this fayth is effectuous through charitie, and expressed in an innocent lyfe.

"OF GOD.

"Of God we byleive in this sorte: that he is almyghtie, beynge one in substance, and thre in persones: which euen as he hathe created by his Worde, that is his Sone, all thynges of nothynge; so by his Spirite and prouydence gouerns he, preserues, and norysheth he, most truly, ryghtously, and wysely all thynges.

" OF MAN.

" Man, whiche is the perfectest image of God in earthe, and also is the chefe dignite and honoure amonge all creatures visible, beynge made of soule and body; of the whiche twayne the body is mortall, the soule immortall ; whan he was creat of God holy, by fallynge in vyce and synne throughe his owne fal, drew with hym in that same ruen and fal, and so subjected all mankynde to the same calamitie and wretchydnes that he fell in.

" OF ORIGINAL SYNNE.

"And so this pestiferous infection whiche men calleth Originall, hathe infecte and ouerspred the whole kynde of man, so far that by no helpe (he beynge the sone of wrathe and vengaunce and enemye of God) coulde be healed by any means but by the helpe of God onely : for yf there be any good that remayneth in man after the fall, that same beynge joyntelie made weaker and weaker by our vyce tournes to the worse ; because the strengthe and power of euyll ouercometh it, and nother suffereth it us to folowe reason nor yet to exersyse the godly-nes of our mynde.

" OF FREWYLL.

" Wherfore we attribute so free wyll to man as we whiche wyttynge and wyllynge to do good, fele experience of euyll. Also euyll trewly we maye do of oure owne wyll, but to embrace and folowe good (except we be elluminat, styred up and mounted, by the grace of Chryst) we maye not : for, ' God is he whiche worketh in us bothe to wyll, to performe, and to accomplyshe for his owne good wyll sake ;' and of God commeth our helth and saluacion, but of our selfe commeth per-dicion.

" OF THE ETERNAL MYNDE OF GOD TO RESTORE MAN.

" And howbeit that through his fault man was subjecte unto dampnacion,' and also was runne under the juste indingnacion of God to take vengeaunce of hym, yet God the father neuer seaced to take a mercyfull care ouer hym : The whiche thynge is manifest not onely of the fyrst promyses and the whole lawe, whiche as it is holy and good, teaching us the wyll of God, ryghtuousnes, and truthe, so worketh it wrath and storeth up synne within us, and slacketh it not, and that not through any faulte of it selfe, but through our vyce, but

E

also clerely appereth it through Christ, whiche was ordayned and geuen for that purpose.

" OF JESUS CHRIST AND THAT IS DONE BY HYM.

" This Christ, the very Sone of God, and very God and very man also, was made our brother, at the tyme appoynted he toke upon him whole man, made of soule and body, hauynge two natures unpermyxte and one dewyne person, to the intent that he shoulde restore unto lyfe us that were deed, and make us aryse of God annexte with hym selfe. He also after that he had taken upon him of the immaculate Virgin, by operacion of the Holy Goost, fleshe, whiche was holy bycause of the union of the Godhed, which is, and also was lyke to our fleshe in all thynges excepte in synfulnes : And that bycause it behoued the sacrefice for synne to be cleane and immaculate, gaue that same fleshe to death for to expell all our synne by that meanes. And he also, to the entent that we shuld have one full and perfecte hope and trust of our immortalitie, hath raysed up agayne fro death to lyfe his owne fleshe, and hath set it and placed it in heauen at the ryghte hande of his Almyghty Father.

" And there he sytteth our victorious champion, our gyder, our capitayne, and heed, also our hyghest bysshop in dede, synne, death, and hell, beynge victoriously ouercome by him, and defendeth oure cause, and pleadeth it perpetually untyll he shall reforme and fascion us to that lykenes to whiche we were create, and brynge us to be partakers of eternall lyfe. And we loke for hym, and beleueth that he shall come at the ende of all ages to be our trewe ryghtuous just Judge, and shall pronounce sentence agaynst all fleshe, whiche shal be raysed up before to that judgement, and that he shall exalte the godly aboue the heauens, but the ungodly shall he condempne bothe body and soule to eternal destruction.

" And as he onely is oure mediatour and entercessour, hoste and sacrifice, bysshop, lorde, and our kynge ; also do we acknowlage and confesse hym onely to be our attonement and raunsome, satisfaction, expiacion, or wysdome, our defence, and our onely deliuerer : refusyng utterly all other meane of lyfe and saluacion, excepte thus by Chryst onely.

" THE ENDE OF THE PREACHYNGE OF THE GOSPELL.

" And therefore in the whole doctryne of the Euangelystes annunciat and shew to be the fyrste, and chefely to be inculcated and taught, that we are safe onely by the marcie of God, and merite of our Sauiour Christ. And that men may perceyue and understande the better, howe necessary is the mercie of God and Christes merites for them, theyr synnes shuld be clerely shewed to them by the lawe, and remission by Christes death.

"OF FAITH AND OF THE POWER OF IT.

" And these so godly benefites, with the very sanctificacion of the Holy Spirite, do we optayne by fayth, the very trewe gyfte of God, and not throughe any other power or strength of ourselues or merytes.

" Whiche faythe is one certayne and undouted substance and aprehensyon of all thynges that we hope for to come of the kyndnes of God, and it cometh firste out of the selfe charitie, it worketh noble frutes of al virtues : yet notwithstandynge we attribute no thyng to the dedes, althoughe they be godly, yet be they mennes workes and actes ; but the helthe and saluacion that is optayned, we attribute to the grace of God onely : And truely this worshypynge alone is the very trewe worshypynge of God ; faythe I meane mooste pryngnaunt and plentifull of good workes, without any confydence in the workes.

"OF THE CONGREGATION OR CHURCHE.

" Also we holde, and belewe, that the Churche, whiche is the congregacion and eleccion of all holy men, whiche also is the spouse of Christ, whom he shall presente without spot unto his Father, washynge it in his owne blode, is of suche lyuely stones aforesayd layde upon this lyuely rock on this maner.

" The whiche Churche, howbeit it be euydently knowne onely to the eyes of God, yet be certayne externall rytes, institute by Christ, and be one publyke and lawful teachynge, teachynge of the Worde of God, not onely as it spyed and knowen, but it is also so constituted by them, that without the cerimonies there is no man reconed to be of it, excepte it be by a synguler preuilege of God.

" THE MINISTERS OF THE WORD OF GOD.

" And for this cause we graunte the Ministers of the Church to be cooperators of God, as Paule calleth them, by whome God geueth and ministreth both knowledge of our selfe, and remission of synne, and conuerteth men to hym selfe, rayseth them up and comforteth them, affrayeth them also, and judgeth them ; but so that the vertue and

efficacie thereof we ascrybe also to the Lorde, and the ministracion of
the sacramentes. For it is manifest that this efficacie and powre is
not bounde nor knytte to any creature, but is dyspensed lyberally and
frely, whosoever, and whensoever, he shall please, for, 'He that
watereth is nothynge, nor yet is he that planteth any thynge, but he
that geueth the encreasment, whiche is God.'

" THE POWER OF THE CHURCHE.

"'The aucthoritie to preache Goddes Worde, and to feede the
Lordes flocke, the whiche properly is the Power of the Keyes, pre-
scribynge and commaundyng all men, bothe hye and lowe, all lyke,
shulde be holy and inuiolat ; and shulde be committed onely to
them that are mete therfore : and chosen other by the eleccion of
God, or elles by a sure and aduysed eleccion of the Churche ; or by
theyr wyll, to whom the Churches depute and apoynt that offyce of
chosynge.

" THE CHOSYNGE OF MINISTERS OR OFFICERS.

" This ministracion and offyce shulde be graunted to no man but
to him whom the ministers of the Churche, and they unto whom the
charge is gyuen by the Churches, and found judged to be of know-
lage in the law of God and of innocent lyfe. The whiche seynge it
is the very eleccion of God, it is well and justlye approued by the
voyce of the Churche, and the imposicion of handes of the heedes of
the preestes.

" THE HEED AND SHEPHERD OF THE CHURCHE.

" Christe, verely, hym selfe is the very trewe heed of his churche
and congregacion, and the onely pastor and heed ; and he also
geueth presydentes, heedes, and teachers, to the entent that in the
externall administracion they shulde use the power of the churche
well and lawfully : Wherfor we knowe not them that are heedes
and pastors in name onely, nor yet the Romenishe heedes.

" THE DUTIE OF MINISTERS OR OFFICERS.

" The chefe and pryncypall offyce of this ministracion is to preache
repentaunce and remission of synne through Jesu Christe ; to praye
continualiy for the people ; to geue diligence wholy to holy stodyes
and to the Worde of God, and resyst and pursue the deuyll alway

with the Word of God, as withe the sworde of the Spirite, and that
with a deadly hatered, and by all meanes to chasten him awaye ; to
defende the holy citezens of Christe. And by all meanes compell and
reproue the fautie and vicious ; and to exclude from the churche
them that stereth to farre, and that by a godly consente and agre-
ment of them whiche are chosen of the ministers and magistrates for
correcyon, or to ponyshe them by any other waye conuenient and
profytable meanes, so longe untyll they come to a mendement, and so
be safe : for this is the returnynge of the churche agayne, for one
suche citizen of Chryst, yf he acknowlage and confesse his erroure
with conuerted mynde and lyfe, for all this doctryne seketh and
wylleth, that we requyre wyllynge and helthefull correccion, exhi-
larite, or comforte all godly by a newe studdy of godlynes.

"OF THE POWER OR STRENGTHE OF SACRAMENTES.

"There is twayne whiche are named in the Church of God Sacramentes, Baptisme, and Howslynge : these be tokens of secrete thynges,
that is, of godly and spirituall thynges, of whiche thynges they take
the name, are not of naked sygnes, but they are of sygnes and verities
together. For in Baptisme the water is the sygne, but the thynge
and verytie is regeneracyon, and adopcion in the people of God. In
the Howslynge and Thankes gyuynge, the bread and the wyne are
sygnes, but the thynge and veritie is the communion of the body of
our Lorde ; helthe and saluacion founde, and remyssyon of synnes ;
the whiche are receyuyed by faythe even as the sygnes and tokens
are receyued by the bodely mouth.

"Wherfore we affyrme the Sacramentes not onely to be badges
and tokens of Christian societie, but to be also sygnes of the grace
of God, by the whiche the ministers worketh withe God, to the ende
that the promyse bryngeth the worke to passe ; but so as is aforesayde of the ministracion of the worde, that all the same powre be
ascribed to the Lorde.

"OF BAPTISM.

"We affyrme Baptism to be by the institucion of the Lorde, the
lauer of regeneracion, the whiche regeneracion the Lorde exhibiteth to
his chosen by a visible sygne by the ministracion of the congregacion, as is aforesayde. In the whiche holy lauer we wasshe oure
infantes, for this cause, because it is wyckednes to rejecte and cast

out of the felowshyp and company of the people of God them that
are borne of us, whiche are the people of God, excepte them that are
expressely commaunded to be rejected by the voyce of God ; and
for this cause chefely, bycause we shulde not presume ungodly of
theyr election.

" OF THE SACRAMENT OF THE AULTER.

" But the misticall supper is in the whiche the Lorde offereth his
body and his blode, that is, his owne selfe, verely, to his owne, for
this entent he myghte lyue more and more in them, and they in hym.
Not so that the body and blode of the Lorde are communed natu-
rally to the bread and wyne, or closed in them as in one place ; or
put in them by any carnal or maruelous presence ; but bycause the
body and blode of oure Lorde are receyued verely of one faythful
soule, and because the bread and the wyne by the institucion of the
Lorde, are tokens be whiche the very communion or participacyon of
the Lordes body and blode are exhibited of the Lorde himselfe,
through the mynistracion of the churche, not to be a meat corruptible
of the body, but to be a noryshemente and meat of eternal lyfe.

" And this holy meat do we use ofte for this cause, for when
through the monicion and rememberaunce of it, we beholde withe the
eye of our fayth the death and blode of hym that was crucified, and
remember oure saluacyon and helthe, not with out a taste of heauenly
lyfe, and very trewe felynge of eternall lyfe : when we do this we are
wonderfully refreshed through this spiritual lyvynge and eternall goode.
And that with an unspeakable swetnes we exulte and rejoyce with a
myrth unexpressable in wordes, for the saluacion that is founde ; and
we all and whole are effused with all our power and strength, utterly
in doynge of thankes for so wonderfull a benefyte of Christ toward
us.

" Therefore it is greatly without oure deservynges that some aleges
and sayeth of us, that we attrybute lyttell to the Holy Sacramentes ;
for they are holy thynges and honourable, bycause they are institute
and ordayned by oure hye preest Christ, and receyued ; exhybiting
the thinges that they syngnifie in theyr owne maner as is aforesayd ;
beynge witnes to the thinge thet is done in dede ; representynge so
hye and harde thynges, and bryngeth by wonderfull corespondence
& lykenes of similitude, a lyght and a clerness to the mynysters
that they sygnifie : so wholy is oure beleve and estimacion of the

Sacramentes, but verely appropriattynge the virtue of quickenynge and santifienge to hym onely whiche is lyfe, to whom be all honour & prayse for ever. Amen.

"OF COMYNGE TO CHURCHE.

"We beleve and thynke the holy conuencions and gatherynges shulde be holden on this maner & sorte: so that fyrst chefely and before all thynges the worde of God be preached to the people openlie in an open & publyke place, and that daylie: and the secrete & obscure places of the Scripture be opened & declared by mete and competent men: And that by the Holy Supper of thankes, called Howselynge, the faithe of the godlie be ofte excreysed, and that they shulde be contynually in prayer for all men & for the necessities of all men. But the rest of the ceremonies which as they are unprofit-able, so are they innumerable, as vescels, garmentes, wax, lyghtes, alters, golde, sylver, in so much as they serve to subverte the trewe religion of God: and chefely Idols & Images that stand open to be worshyped, and geve offence & slaunder; and all suche prophane and ungodlie thynges do we abandon, reject, & put away from the holy congregacion & conuencion.

"OF HERETYCKES & SYSMATTYCKES.

"We also abandon & reject from our holy conuencions all them that departeth from the societe & fellowship of the holy Churche, and bryngeth in straunge or ungodlie sectes and opinions. With the whiche evyll the Anabaptistes are chefly infecte this tyme: the whiche we judge shuld be constrayned and punished by the majestrates and hye powers, yf they obstinatly do resyst and wyll not obeye the monission of the Church, and that for the intent that they shulde not infecte and corrupt the flocke of God through theyr wycked evyll.

"OF THYNGES INDYFFERENT.

"The thynges that are called, and in dede also are indifferent, howbeit a godlie man may use them frely, and in every place, and at all tymes, yet notwythstandynge he shulde use them with know-lage and of charitie to the glory of God trewly, and the edificacion of the Churche and congregacion.

" OF MAGISTRATES OR GOUERNOURS.

" And seynge euery magistrate and hyghe powre is of God, his chefe and pryncipall office is (excepte he wolde rather use tyranny) to defende the trewe worshipinge of God from all blasfemy and to pro- cure trewe religion, and as the prophete doth teache of the voyce of God, to execute for his powre. In whiche part a trewe and syncere preachinge of the worde of God remayneth with a ryghte and dili- gente institucion of the discipline of citezens, and of the scooles : just correcion and nurture, with liberalitie towarde the mynysters of the Churche with a solicitat and thoughtfull charge of the poore, to the whiche ende all the rychesse of the Churche is referred. This, I saye, hathe the fyrst and chefe place in the execution of the magistrat.

" Then after to judge the people by equall and godlie lawes, to exersyce and mayntayne judgment & justice, to defend the comune- welthe, and punishe transgressours accordynge to theyr faulte, outher in goodes, theyr bodies or theyr lyves. And when the majestrate executeth these thynges he honoreth God as he shulde, in his voca- cion, and we (howbeit we be free bothe in our body and in all oure goodes, and in the studies of oure minde and thought also, with a trewe faithe) knoweth that we shulde be subjecte in holynes to the majestrate and shulde keep fydelitie and promes to hym, so long as his commandmentes, statutes and imperes evidently repugneth not with Him for whose sake we honour and worship the majestrates.

" OF HOLY MATRIMONY.

" We judge Mariage, whiche was instytute of God for all men, apte and mete therfor, which are not called from it by any other vocation, to repugn holyness of no ordre ; the whiche mariage as the Churche auctoriseth it & celebrates, so solempniseth it with orison & prayer.   And therefor we rejecte & refuse this monckly chastite, and all & hole this slouthful & sluggish sorte of lyfe of supersticious men, as abominablye invented & excogitat thynge, and abandon it as a thinge repugnant bothe to the comune weale & to the Churche.   And so confirmeth and stablesseth it, so it belongeth to the magistrate to se that it be worthely bothe begoune & worshypped ; & not broken but for a just cause.

" A DECLARACION OR WYTNESSYNGE OF OURE MINDE.

" It is not oure mynde for to prescribe by this breefe chapters a certayne rule of the Faythe to all Churches & congregacyones, for we know no outher rule of faythe but the Holy Scripture. And therefore we are well contented with them that agreeth with these thynges, howbeit they use ane other maner of speakinge, or Confession dyfferent apartly to this of ours in wordes, for rather shulde the matter be consydered then the wordes. And therefore we make it free for all men to use theyr owne sorte of speakynge, as they shall perceyue most profitable for theyr churches and we shall use the same libertie. And yf any man wyll attempte to corrupte the trewe meanynge of this oure Confession, he shall heare both a confession and a defence of the veritie and truth.

" It was oure pleasure to use these wordes at this present tyme that we myght declare our opinion in our religion & worshipenge of God.

" FINIS.

" *The Truth wyl have the upper hande.*"

GENEALOGICAL HISTORY OF THE
HOUSE OF WISHART.

NISBET'S statement as to the family of Wishart having derived descent from Robert, an illegitimate son of David, Earl of Huntingdon, who was styled Guishart on account of his heavy slaughter of the Saracens, is an evident fiction.*

The name Guiscard, or Wiscard, a Norman epithet used to designate an adroit or cunning person, was conferred on Robert Guiscard, son of Tancrede de Hauterville of Normandy, afterwards Duke of Calabria, who founded the kingdom of Sicily. This noted warrior died on the 27th July 1085. His surname was adopted by a branch of his House, and the name became common in Normandy and throughout France. Guiscard was the surname of the Norman kings of Apulia in the twelfth and thirteenth centuries.

John Wychard is mentioned as a small landowner in the Hundred de la Mewe, Buckinghamshire, in the reign of Henry III. (1216-1272).† During the same reign and that of Edward I. (1272-1307), are named as landowners, Baldwin Wyschard or Wistchart, in Shropshire ; Nicholas Wychard, in Warwickshire ; Hugh Wischard, in Essex ; and William Wischard, in Bucks.‡ In the reign of Edward I. Julian Wyechard is named as occupier of a house in the county of Oxford.§

A branch of the House of Wischard obtained lands in Scotland some time prior to the thirteenth century. John Wischard was sheriff of Kincardineshire in the reign of Alexander II. (1214-1249). In an undated charter of this monarch, Walter of Lundyn, and Christian his wife, grant

---

* Nisbet's System of Heraldry, Edin., 1816, folio, vol. i., p. 201.
† Rotuli Hundredorum, vol. i.   ‡ Testa. de Nevill, *passim.*
§ Rotuli Hundredorum, vol. ii., p. 727.

to the monks of Arbroath a chalder of grain, "pro sua frater-
nitate," the witnesses being John Wischard, "vicecomes de
Moernes," and his son John.* John Wischard is witness to a
charter, by Stephen de Kinardley, granting to the church of
St Thomas the Martyr, of Arbroath, the davach of land in
Kincardineshire called Petmengartenach. This charter is
undated, but as it contains the names of Alexander II. and
his queen Johanna, it evidently belongs to the period between 1221 and 1249.† " J. Wischard vicecomes de Mernez "
and John, his son, are witnesses to a charter by Robert
Warnebald and Richenda his spouse, granting to the kirk of
St Thomas of Arbroath, all their fief (feodum) in the parish
of Fordun, comprising the two Tubertachthas, Glenferkeryn,
Kynkell, and Kulback and Monbodachyn.‡ This instrument
is undated, but there follows a charter of confirmation by
Alexander II., dated 20th March, in the twenty-fourth year
of his reign (1238).

John Wischart, sheriff of the Mearns, or Kincardineshire,
was father of three sons. William, the second son, entered the
Church. Possessing superior abilities and extensive culture,
he became Archdeacon of St Andrews, and while holding that
office was, in 1256, appointed chancellor of the kingdom. He
was, in 1270, elected Bishop of Glasgow, but in the same year
was postulated to St Andrews.§ By the decree of Pope
Urban IV., every bishop-elect was required to proceed to
Rome for consecration, and Gregory X., the reigning pontiff,
insisted that this rule should be obeyed. Disinclined to
undertake the long and perilous journey, Bishop Wishart despatched agents to Rome, begging that he might receive consecration at home. After a long detention, the agents were
informed that the papal sanction would be withheld ; but, on
the persuasion of Edward I., who was then at Rome, on his
way from Palestine, the pontiff consented to grant the necessary letters.‖ In 1274 Bishop Wishart was consecrated at

* Reg. Vetus de Aberbrothoc, p. 97.   † Ib., p. 179.   ‡ Ib., pp. 198, 199.
§ Fordun, lib. x., p. 133.
‖ Spottiswoode's History, Edin., 1851, 3 vols. 8vo, vol. i., p. 91.

Scone, in presence of the king, several bishops, and many of
the nobility.   He thereupon resigned his office of chancellor.*

Along with other prelates of the Scottish Church, Bishop
Wishart attended a Council held at Lyons in 1274, when a
union was effected with the Eastern Church, and decrees were
passed for reducing the mendicant orders, and abolishing
pluralities.   The two latter reforms were practically un-
availing, for, by payments at the court of Rome, mendicant
monks were allowed to beg as before, and ambitious clerks
were permitted to hold as many benefices as they could procure.   In 1275, Bagimund, a papal nuncio, arrived in Scotland, and, at a council held at Perth, fixed the value of Scottish benefices.†   The revenues of the bishopric of St Andrews
were estimated at an amount equal to £9450 of sterling money.

Commended by the chronicler, Wyntoun, Bishop William
Wischart is by the historian, John of Fordoun, denounced as
a pluralist and charged with hypocrisy.‡   Whatever may
have been his private character, his public acts bespeak his
praise, for, during the seven years he held his bishopric, he
founded at St Andrews the elegant structure of the Dominican monastery, and in superb architecture reared the nave
of the cathedral.§   While engaged with other leading persons in settling the vexed question of the marches between
the kingdoms, he was seized with a mortal ailment, and
expired at Morebattle in 1278.   His remains were conveyed
to St Andrews, and there deposited in the cathedral, near the
high altar.‖

Adam, third son of John Wishart, sheriff of the Mearns,
had, in 1272, a charter of the lands of Ballandarg and Logie,
in the county of Forfar, from Gilbert de Umphraville, Earl of
Angus, and a crown charter confirming the same, dated 13th

---

* Spottiswoode's History, Edin., 1851, 3 vols. 8vo, vol. i., p. 92.

† The table, commonly called Bagiment's Roll, served as a rule for the prices
taken of those who came to sue for benefices at the court of Rome (Spottiswoode's History, vol. i., p. 93).

‡ Fordun's Scotichronicon, lib. x., c. 28.

§ Wyntoun's Chronicle, Edin., 1872, vol. ii., p. 258.

‖ Spottiswoode's History, vol. i., p. 93 ; Wyntoun, vol. ii., p. 250.

July 1280, in which he is styled "Adam Wyschard, filius Joannis." In 1279 he received from William, Abbot of Arbroath, a charter of the lands of Kenny-Murchardyn, or Kennyneil, in the parish of Kingoldrum, Forfarshire.* From him descended the House of Wishart of Logie Wishart, otherwise the Wisharts of that ilk. To this branch we shall refer subsequently.

Sir John Wishart, eldest son of John Wischart, sheriff of the Mearns, obtained the lands of Conveth (Laurencekirk), Halkertoun, and Scottistoun, in the Mearns, from Adam, Abbot of Arbroath. Of these lands he had a charter of confirmation, dated 21st June 1246, wherein he is designed "Johannes Wyscard, filius Johannis." By a legal instrument addressed to the Abbot of Arbroath, he became bound not to alienate any portion of his lands without the abbot's consent.† This instrument is undated, but appears to belong to the year 1260. He was knighted by Alexander II., and, as Sir John Wishart, is a witness to the foundation charter of the hospital of Brechin.‡

On the death of Sir John Wishart, which took place in the reign of Alexander III., he was succeeded by his eldest son, also Sir John. This baron, along with his son John, took the oath of fealty to Edward I. at Elgin on the 29th July 1296.§ During the same year he granted ten merks out of the lands of Redhall and Balfeith, for support of the chapel of St Thomas the Martyr, in the cathedral of Brechin.‖ He died at an advanced age.

In a charter by Margaret, Countess of Douglas, Lady Mar and Garioch, dated Feast of the Assumption, 1384, John Wischard is witness to the resignation in her hands of the lands of Colchill and Petgoury.¶

In 1391 Robert III. prohibited Sir William of Keth, sheriff

---

* Dalrymple's Historical Collections, Edin., 1705, p. 217; Reg. Vet. de Aberd., 332; Jervise's Angus and Mearns, p. 347.

† Reg. Vet. de Aberbrothoc, *passim.*   ‡ Reg. Epis. Brechin., vol. i., p. 7.

§ Ragman Roll, pp. 103, 109.   ‖ Reg. Epis. Brechin., vol. i., pp. 59-61.

¶ Reg. Epis. Aberd., p. 331.

of Kincardineshire, from enforcing payment of certain fines, which the men of Sir John Wishart were adjudged to pay in the last justiciary circuit held within his baliary—these fines amounting to £14.*

Sir John Wishart, the fifth baron of certain lands in Kincardineshire, is the first of his House styled of Pitarrow. As "Dominus Joannes Wishart de Pittarro," he, in 1399, entered into an indenture with John, Abbot of Arbroath, respecting the mill and mill lands of Conveth. He died early in the reign of James I., leaving a son, who succeeded to his estate.

Sir John Wischart, second of Pitarrow, went to France in the suite of the Princess Margaret, when, in 1434, she was married to the Dauphin, afterwards Louis XI.† In 1437 £8 were allocated for the farms of the lands of Gurdnes, part of the manor of Firmartin, granted by the king to Sir John Wishart.‡ On the 6th July 1442, "Sir John Wyschart, lord of Pettarrow, knight," appeared before the chapter of Brechin, and to the vicar-general, in the absence of the bishop, presented "Schir David Wyschart" as his chaplain, endowing him with ten merks of annual rent from certain lands.§ Having founded, with an endowment of ten merks yearly, from the lands of Redhall and others, the chaplainry of St Thomas the Martyr, in the cathedral of Brechin, for the salvation of his soul, and that of Janet (Ochterlony), his wife, he, on the 10th of August 1442, presented as chaplain "his well-beloved David Wyschart, to be admitted thereto after examination."‖ In an instrument dated 17th November 1453, David Wyschard is mentioned as one of the vicars or perpetual chaplains of the church of Brechin.¶

In 1447 Alexander Wishart of Pitarrow witnesses the resignation by William Fullerton of the lands of Maryton.** James Wishart of Pitarrow, who had probably succeeded to

* Rotuli Compotorum in Scaccaris, vol. ii., p. 177.
† Chamberlain Rolls, ii. 117, iii. 367.
‡ Rotuli Compotorum in Scaccaris, vol. iii., p. 366.
§ Reg. Epis. Brechin., p. 58.   ‖ Ib., p. 59.
* Ib., p. 96.   ** Ib., ii. 63.

the estate as a younger brother, obtained on the 17th January
1461, a charter from the Abbot of Arbroath, of the mill and
mill lands of Conveth. This instrument William Ochterlony
of Kelly, designed uncle of James Wishart, subscribed as a
witness. In 1471 James Wishart of Pitarrow is mentioned as
holding the Constable lands of Brechin. In connection with
these lands he is named in a charter dated 30th March 1482.*
He died in June 1491, leaving a son John, and a daughter
Marjory. The latter married Gilbert Middleton of that ilk.
In the "Acta Auditorum" of 1493 there is a decree respecting
the settlement of her dowry.

John Wishart of Pitarrow did homage, on the 25th February 1492, to Robert Leighton, Abbot of Arbroath, for his
lands of Reidhall and others. In June 1493 he is mentioned
in a decreet of the Lords of Council.† In 1499 he appears
to have suffered forfeiture, when his lands of Balgillo were
granted to others. He married a daughter of Janet, daughter
of Lyndsay of Edzell, with whom he got a charter, under the
Great Seal, of the lands of Woodtoun and others in the
county of Kincardine.

By his wife Janet Lyndsay, John Wishart of Pitarrow had
three sons, James, John, and William. John, the second son,
along with his elder brother James, entered into an agree-
ment respecting certain lands and other property, on the 19th
March 1508. William, the third son, described as brother-
german of the deceased "Master James Wyshart of Pitarrow,"
had, on the 28th October 1525, a grant from the Abbot of
Arbroath of the ward and relief of his brother's lands. James
Wishart, eldest son of John Wishart, had, as his first wife,
Janet Lyndsay. On the 28th October 1510, a precept was
granted by the Abbot of Arbroath for infefting him and
"Janet Lyndsay his spouse" in the lands of Redhall, Balfeith, and others, which belonged to his father, John Wishart
of Pitarrow. On the 11th August 1511, he obtained a charter
under the Great Seal of the lands of Carncbege, in the county
of Kincardine. By James IV. he was appointed "Justice

* Reg. Epis. Brechin., ii. 117.   † Acts of Lords of Council, 1466-1494.

Clerk * and King's Advocate " in December 1513, offices
which he retained till some time between the years 1520
and 1524. He was a member of the General Council which
was held at Perth on the 26th November 1513, to meet
Monsieur Labatie and Mr James Ogilvy, ambassadors from
Louis XII., to confer respecting the renewal of the French
league and the return of the Duke of Albany.† On the
13th November 1516, he had a charter of the lands of Easter
and Wester Howlands, Howlawshead, and others. He died
before May 1525.

Subsequent to the 28th October 1510, and the 30th April
1512, James Wishart married as his second wife Elizabeth
Learmont, a daughter or near relation of James Learmont of
Balcomie, in Fife. On the 30th April 1512, he received,
along with " Elizabeth Learmont his spouse," a royal charter
of the lands of Easter and Wester Pitarrow, on the resignation of his father, John Wishart of Pitarrow, reserving to his
father, and Janet Lyndsay his spouse, their " frank tenement
of the said lands during their lives."‡ Of his first marriage
were born two sons, John and James, and two daughters,
Janet and another; of the second a son George, the future
martyr.

Janet, daughter of James Wishart of Pitarrow by his first
marriage, espoused James Durham of Pitkerrow. His other
daughter married George Leslie, third laird of Pitnamoon, by
whom she had an only daughter.§

John, eldest son of James Wishart of Pitarrow, held a portion of his lands from the Abbey of Arbroath. Of that
abbey, David Beaton, the future cardinal, became commendator in 1524. On the 10th May 1525, Beaton, as Abbot of
Arbroath, directed to James Strachan of Monboddo, and
others, a precept for infefting John Wishart as heir to his
father, James Wishart of Pitarrow, in the mill and lands of
Conveth (Laurencekirk), held by the abbey in chief. This

* Clerk of the Justiciary Court.   † Acta Parl. Scot., vol. ii.
‡ Reg. Mag. Sig., lib. xviii., No. 44.
§ Colonel Leslie's Family of Leslie, vol. ii., p. 150.

precept is not, according to usage, sealed with the official seal of the abbey, but with the abbot's private seal, on which his family arms are engraved. Beaton also attaches his signature, thus : *

On the 9th February 1531, John Wishart of Pitarrow obtained a gift of the ward of the lands of Wester Glenburny and others in the county of Kincardine, which belonged to the late James Wishart of Pitarrow, and Elizabeth Learmont his spouse, conjunct fiar thereof—the dues of which were in the king's hand.†

John Wishart died unmarried, or without issue. James, his younger brother, styled "of Carnebege," in the parish of Fordoun,‡ married, and had four sons, John, James, Alexander, and George ; and two daughters, Margaret and Christina.

Margaret Wishart married, first, William Gardyne, younger of Burrofield, and, secondly, in 1560, Alexander Tullo, son of William Tullo, younger of Craignestoun.§ Christina Wishart married John Wedderburn, burgess of Dundee. On the 29th May 1571, sasine was granted on a precept by Patrick Kinnaird of that ilk, in favour of Christina Wishart, relict of the late John Wedderburn, burgess of Dundee, in liferent ; and to George Wishart, "armigero crucis christianissimi regis Galliæ," her brother, of an annual rent of £20 Scots, furth of the corn mill of Kinnaird.‖ Alexander, third son of John Wishart of Pitarrow, married Marion, daughter of Alexander Falconer of Halkerton. On the 2d October 1556, he received precept of a royal charter for confirming him in a portion of

* Fraser's Earls of Southesk, pp. lxv., lxvi.
† Reg. Sec. Sig., vol. ix., fol. 76.   ‡ Ib., vol. xxvii., fol. 51.
§ Matrimonial Contract in Register of Deeds, dated 8th February 1560.
‖ Protocol Register of Thomas Ireland, Notary Public, in the Town-Clerk's Office, Dundee.

F

the lands of Halkerton, granted him by Alexander Falconer.* He was, on the 1st February 1562, appointed captain and keeper "of the houses, place, and fortalice of Badgenocht and bailie of the lands, barony, and bounds of the same."† From Sir John Wishart, his eldest brother, he received, on the 24th May 1566, precept of a charter of the lands of Carnebeg,‡ in the county of Kincardine, which lands were further destined to his brother George.§

George Wishart, fourth son of John Wishart of Pitarrow, obtained military employment in France. On the 14th June 1565, sasine proceeded on a charter granted by John Wallace of Craigie, in favour of "George Wischart, brother-german of John Wischart of Pitarrow, *armiger crucis regis Galliæ*." By this charter George Wishart received the lands of Westerdoid, in the lordship of Murlachewod and shire of Forfar. The charter is dated 5th June 1565, and on behalf of George Wishart sasine is granted in the hands of his attorney, described as "George Wishart of Drymme." George Wishart of Westerdoid died unmarried. On the 5th March 1573, he nominated his sister, Christina Wishart, relict of John Wedderburn, his cessioner, or residuary legatee. ‖

John, eldest son of James Wishart of Carnebeg, and grandson of the justice-clerk, succeeded John Wishart, his uncle, in the lands and barony of Pitarrow. On the 3d October 1545, he received a gift of the non-entries of the lands of Staddokmure, otherwise Reidheuch, and others, in the county of Kincardine, which were held by Queen Mary, by reason of non-entry, since the death of umquhile ——— Strachan.¶ On the 24th March 1553, a precept of charter was granted to John Wishart, "son and heir of the late James Wishart,"

---

* Reg. Sec. Sig., vol. xxviii., fol. 94b. † *Ib.*, vol. xxxviii., fol. 31.

‡ Members of the family of Wishart, chiefly engaged in agricultural pursuits, resided at Carnebeg, in the parish of Fordoun, till the middle of the eighteenth century; they are represented by the Rev. James Wishart, pastor of Toxteth Church, Liverpool.

§ Reg. Sec. Sig., vol. xxxv., fol. 35.

‖ Protocol Book of Thomas Ireland, in Town-Clerk's Office, Dundee.

¶ Reg. Sec. Sig., vol. xix., fol. 43.

of the lands of Bathaggarties and others, in the lordship of Mar.*

John Wishart engaged, like his grandfather, in legal studies. While prosecuting these studies at Edinburgh, it is believed that, through Learmont of Balcomie, he became acquainted with Crichton of Brunstone, Norman Leslie, and others, who were concerned in a plot against Cardinal Beaton. In connection with this conspiracy he, in April 1544, acted as messenger between Crichton and the English court. After succeeding to the paternal estates in 1545, he seems to have withdrawn from public affairs till 1557, when he joined the Earls of Argyle and Glencairn, Lord James Stuart, Prior of St Andrews, and John Erskine of Dun, in despatching a communication to John Knox at Geneva, inviting him to return to Scotland, and assuring him of general support. This communication was dated 10th March 1557 ; and on receiving it Knox at once undertook his journey homeward. But at Dieppe, which he reached in October, he was informed by other correspondents that the zeal of the Scottish Reformers had considerably waned, and that few would imperil their fortunes by attempting a change. Knox was much disheartened, and determined to return to Geneva. Before leaving Dieppe he addressed letters of exhortation to the leading Reformers, and private communications to the Lairds of Pitarrow and Dun.

On receiving Knox's private letters, Wishart and Erskine called together the leading Reformers, and urged them to immediate action. The result was that, on the 3d December 1557, was framed that memorable bond by which the Reformers confederated under the name of the Congregation, each becoming bound to seek the destruction of the Romish Church.† Of the Congregation Wishart continued one of the leading members. When, on the 24th May 1559, they met at Perth, to devise measures for resisting the queen regent, Wishart and Erskine were deputed to assure the

* Reg. Sec. Sig., vol. xxvii., fol. 51.
† Knox's History, edit. 1846, vol. i., pp. 267-274, 337-350, 361-451.

royal envoys that, while they cherished no disloyal intentions, they would firmly assert their privileges. On the 4th June Wishart and Erskine attended a conference at St Andrews, with the Earl of Argyle and Lord James Stuart, who acted as representatives of the regent. Of this conference the result was favourable to the Reformed cause, and Knox at once commenced his public exposure of Romish error. The first day's preaching at St Andrews was followed by a popular insurrection, and the wrecking of the Dominican and Franciscan monasteries.

The queen regent having at length consented to grant to the body of the Congregation freedom of worship, Wishart joined a deputation in opening with her negotiations for this purpose, but the crafty princess withdrew her pledge. Wishart, with others, resented her duplicity by subscribing a manifesto declaring that she had forfeited her office as regent. He attended the convention at Berwick in February 1560, when the Duke of Norfolk, on behalf of Queen Elizabeth, agreed to support the Congregation against the power of France ; * and when the English army reached Edinburgh in April, with the intention of expelling the French, he joined the nobility and barons in hailing their advent, and pledging cordial co-operation.†

In the Parliament held at Edinburgh on the 1st August 1560, John Wishart of Pitarrow is named as one of the commissioners of burghs. By this Parliament, on the 17th August, the Confession of Faith was ratified.‡ The government of the State was entrusted to twenty-four persons, eight of whom were to be chosen by the queen, and six by the nobility. Wishart was one of those selected by the nobles.§

With a view to the surrender, by the Romish clergy, of the third portion of their revenues, Wishart was, in 1561, appointed, along with certain officers of state, to prepare a valuation of ecclesiastical property.‖ On the 8th February 1561-2,

---

* Knox's History, edit. 1846, vol. ii., pp. 45-52.　　† Ib., pp. 61-64.

‡ Acta Parl. Scot., vol. ii., p. 526.　　§ Keith's History, p. 152.

‖ Knox's History, vol. ii., p. 304.

when the Earl of Murray (Lord James Stuart) was married
to Agnes Keith, daughter of the Earl Marischal, he was,
along with nine other notable persons, honoured with knighthood.*   On the 15th February he was appointed Comptroller
and Collector - General of Teinds.†   In this capacity he
became paymaster of the Reformed clergy.   These bitterly
complained of their scanty incomes, and Knox relates that
the saying prevailed, "The good Laird of Pitarro was ane
earnest professor of Christ ; but the mekle Devill receave the
Comptroller."‡

At the battle of Corrichie, fought on the 5th November
1562, between the followers of the rebel Earl of Huntly and
the royal troops, Sir John Wishart was present and highly
distinguished himself.§   In the Parliament held at Edinburgh
on the 4th June 1563, he was appointed with others to decide
as to those who should have the benefit of the Act of Oblivion,
for offences committed from the 6th March 1558 to the 1st
September 1560.‖

Actively employed in the State, Sir John Wishart did not
overlook family affairs.   On the 21st December 1557, he and
his wife, Janet Falconer, received a third part of the lands of
Halkerton.   He, on the 21st September 1563, had the precept
of a charter of the lands of Enrowglass, in the lordship of
Badenoch and sheriffdom of Inverness.*   On the 23d January 1564, he received a charter of the lands of Glenmuick,
Assynt, Glentanner, Inchmarno, Tullych, Ballater, and others
in the county of Aberdeen.**   By a letter under the Privy
Seal he was granted, on the 24th May 1565, the reversion of
the lands and barony of Rothiemurchus, in the regality of
Spynie and sheriffdom of Inverness, escheat by the treason
of the Lord Gordon.††   On the 28th July 1565, he and his
wife obtained a precept of charter, in conjunct fee, of the lands

* Knox's History, vol. ii., p. 314, note by Mr David Laing.
† Reg. Sec. Sig., vol. xxxi., Nos. 3 and 5.
‡ Knox's History, vol. ii., pp. 310, 311.   § Ib., vol. ii., p. 356.
‖ Acta Parl. Scot., vol. ii., p. 536.   ¶ Reg. Sec. Sig., vol. xxxii., No. 4.
** Ib., No. 1316.   †† Ib., vol. xxxiii., No. 48.

of Easter and Wester Balfour and Incharbak, in the county of Kincardine.*

Having joined the Earl of Murray in opposing the marriage of Queen Mary with Lord Darnley, Sir John was denounced a rebel, and obliged to seek refuge in England. Consequent on his forfeiture, the rents owing him by Mr George Gordon of Balderny were, on the 26th October 1565, granted to Mr John Gordon ;† and a debt of 300 merks owing him by Captain Alexander Crichton of Hallyard was presented to the debtor.‡ By a letter under the Privy Seal Walter Wood of Balbirgenocht obtained the rents of his lands of Pitarrow, Easter Pitarrow, Wester Mill of Petreny, Pettingard-nave, Little Carnebeg, Reidhall, Easter Wottoun, Wester Wottoun, Easter Balfour, Wester Balfour, Incheharbertt, Gallowhilton, and Crofts of Kincardine, with the lands of Glentanner and Braes of Mar.§

Sir John Wishart returned to Scotland after the slaughter of David Rizzio. That event took place on the 9th March 1566, and on the 21st day of the same month, he obtained the royal pardon for "participating with the Duke of Chatelherault and Arran, Lord Hamilton, in holding the castles of Hamilton and Draffan on the 30th September last." ‖ On the 24th May 1566, he granted a precept of charter of the lands of Carnebeg, in the county of Kincardine, to his brother-german, Alexander Wishart of Cosvell, and Marion Falconer, his wife, whom failing, to George Wishart, his brother-german.¶

In 1567 Sir John Wishart received a royal precept for confirming a charter of alienation by James, Earl of Murray, of the lands of Cragane, Cambusnakist, Auchin-dryne, Auchquhillater, Kyndrocht, and others in the lordship of Braemar.** The right of Sir John to the possession of these lands was disputed by the Earl of Mar, who brought his claim under the consideration of Parliament. On the

---

* Reg. Sec. Sig., vol. xxxiii., No. 95b.   † Ib., No. 115b.
‡ Ib., No. 122.   § Ib., vol. xxxv., No. 456.   ‖ Ib., No. 12b.
¶ Ib., No. 35.   ** Ib., vol. xxxviii., No. 31.

29th July 1567, the Estates of Parliament recommended a private settlement.*

In May 1567, Sir John joined the confederacy against the Earl of Bothwell. He was, on the 19th November of the same year, appointed an extraordinary Lord of Session.†
In 1568 he accompanied the Regent Murray to York, and gave his sanction to the charges preferred against Queen Mary.‡

After the battle of Langside, and the assumption of the regency by the Duke of Chatelherault (formerly known as the Regent Arran), Sir John Wishart attached himself to the duke's party in opposition to his former friend and patron, the Regent Murray. In the cause of Queen Mary, he joined Sir William Kirkaldy in the Castle of Edinburgh, and became constable of the fort. He was one of eight persons by whose assistance Kirkaldy undertook to hold the castle against all assailants.§ When Kirkaldy capitulated in May 1573, he became a prisoner in the hands of the Regent Morton. On the 11th July, he was denounced a rebel, and his lands and goods were conferred on his nephew, "Mr John Wishart, son to Mr James Wishart of Balfeith."‖ He was also deprived of his office of judge. On the 18th January 1574, he was re-appointed an extraordinary Lord of Session.¶ He died on the 25th September 1576.** Sir John married Janet, sister of Sir Alexander Falconer of Halkerton, but had no children.

James Wishart, second son of John Wishart of Pitarrow and brother of Sir John Wishart, received, on the 14th April 1545, from Cardinal Beaton as Commendator of Arbroath, a precept for infefting him and Elizabeth Wood,†† his spouse,

* Acta Parl. Scot., vol. iii., pp. 476-478.
† Pitmedden MS.
‡ Memoirs of Sir James Melvil, p. 186.
§ Spottiswoode's History, Edin., 1851, vol. ii., p. 193; Melvil's Memoirs, p. 241.
‖ Reg. Sec. Sig., vol. xli., No. 90b.
¶ Brunton and Haig's Senators of the College of Justice, p. 138.
** Knox's History, ed. 1846, vol. ii., p. 311, note by Mr David Laing.
†† This gentlewoman was probably a daughter of David Wood of Craig, who

in the town and lands of Balfeith, in the barony of Redhall, regality of Arbroath, and shire of Kincardine. The precept bears that the lands formerly belonged to John Wishart of Pitarrow, and were resigned by him into the cardinal's hands; it is dated at the monastery of Arbroath, and subscribed by the cardinal and twenty-one of the brethren convened in chapter. It is impressed with the round seal of the cardinal, and counter-sealed with his privy seal ; it also bears the common seal of the abbey.*

James Wishart of Balfeith died in April 1575. In his will, which was executed on the 24th April of that year, he names three sons, John, James, and Alexander, and five daughters, Elspit, Christian, Jane, Isobel,† and Helen. His brother, Alexander, styled "of Carnebeg," subscribes as one of the witnesses, and Sir John Wishart, his eldest brother, is constituted "oversman" of his executors.‡

John Wishart, eldest son of James Wishart of Balfeith, succeeded to the lands and barony of Pitarrow on the death of his uncle, Sir John Wishart, in September 1576. In a Parliament held at Stirling in 1578, of which he was a member, John Wishart of Pitarrow was nominated one of the commissioners for examining the "Buik of the Policy of the Kirk," with a view to its public ratification.§ On the 16th February 1585, he was served heir to Sir John Wishart in the lands of Cairnton and others, and in Fordoun, a free burgh of barony.‖ In 1587 he awakened a legal process against the Countess of Murray "for execution of a decreet of warrandice" upon the lands of Strathtie and Braemar, granted to Sir John by the Regent Earl of Murray. In 1592 he was

was Comptroller from 1538 to 1546 (Sir John Scot's Staggering State, Edin., 1872, p. 111, note by Goodal).

* Fraser's Earls of Southesk, pp. lxv., lxvi.

† Isobel Wishart, Prioress of the Grey Sisters at Dundee, received on the 16th May 1566 the gift of a nun's portion, "with chalmer, habite, silver, fyre, candill, and all other thinges necessare within the Abbey of North Berwick" (Reg. Sec. Sig., vol. xxxv., p. 46).

‡ Edin. Com. Reg., *Testaments*, vol. iv.

§ Acta Parl. Scot., vol. iii., p. 105.   ‖ Inq. Spec., Kincardine, No. 4.

allowed by Parliament to proceed against the heirs of the Earl of Murray, but at a Parliament held at Edinburgh on the 8th June 1594, the proceedings were arrested on the grounds that the earl was under age, that the documents on which his defence rested were burned at Donibristle when the late earl was murdered, and that the estates of the earldom were heavily encumbered.*

In 1592 Sir John Wishart of Pitarrow "subscribed the band anent religion at Aberdeen." He was in the same year appointed one of the Earl Marischal's deputies, to apprehend the Earl of Huntly and others, for the burning of Donibristle, and murder of the Earl of Murray. He married Jean, daughter of William Douglas, ninth Earl of Angus. A charter under the Great Seal, "Domino Joanni Wishart de Pittarro et Dominæ Jeannæ Douglas ejus spousæ baroniarum de Pittarro, Reidhall, etc.," is dated 7th April 1603. Of this marriage were born four sons, John, James, William, and Alexander, and a daughter, Elizabeth, who married Sir William Forbes, Bart. of Monymusk. Sir John Wishart died at an advanced age before the 30th April 1607. According to Sir John Scot he lived to "a good age in good reputation." †

John Wishart, eldest son of Sir John Wishart of Pitarrow, had at the university as his companion, John Gordon, afterwards Dean of Salisbury. This divine dedicated to him in 1603 his "Assertiones Theologicæ," ‡ in these commendatory terms:

"*Nobili & generoso juueni* JOANNI SOPHOCARDIO *Pittarroensi, Joannes Gordonius Brittanno-Scotus, S. P. D.*

"Hisce diebus elapsis (Sophocardi amicissime) dū animi oblectandi gratiâ musæolum nostrum inuiseres, de controuersijs religionis nostri

---

* Acta Parl. Scot., vol. iv., p. 80.

† Scot's Staggering State, Edin., 1872, p. 111.

‡ The full title is, "Assertiones Theologicæ pro vera veræ Ecclesiæ Nota, quæ est solius Dei Adoratio : contra falsæ Ecclesiæ Creaturarum Adorationem. Rupell, 1603." The work is extremely rare. A copy is preserved in the Bodleian Library.

sæculi agere cœpisti, & argumenta in medium proponere quibus
nituntur nostrates pontificis Romani emissarij animum tuum ad
Romana deliria allicere, quæ pro tenuitate mea diluere sategi
hinc mihi in animum venit breuiusculas assertiones ex
lucubrationib. nostris Theologicis colligere, per quas rationibus
solidissimis euincimus Episcopos & doctores pontificios in Gen-
tilium, Arrianorum, Nestorianorum, & Eutychianorum errores
blasphemos dilapsos esse, adeò vt externæ ordinationis Episcopalis
character, quem superbè jactitant, per doctrinæ corruptelam irritus
& inanis euasit ; ac proinde nullam veræ Ecclesiæ notam reliquam
penes aulæ Romanæ adulatores permansisse. Tu verò pro ingenitâ
animi tui sinceritate & zelo gloriæ Dei efflagitasti vt has easdem
assertiones in publicam Ecclesiæ Dei vtilitatem emitterem, vt illis
adolescentium nostratium animi præmuniantur, tanquam amuleto
contra Idolomaniam pontificiam, quæ passim grassatur, & in-
numeram mortalium multitudinem ad animarum naufragium impellit,
dū splendore honorum & diuitiarum fulgore mentis oculos illis
perstringit, vt caduca bona solidis & æternis anteferant.   Accipe
ergo, mi Sophocardi, has assertiones quibus conficiendis ansam
præbuisti, vt non tibi solum, sed & Christianis omnibus qui seruari
expetunt prosint : & memoriam Georgij Sophocardij patrui tui
magni in scrinio pectoris reconde ; qui pro veritate Christianâ fortiter
strenuèq dimicans, impiâ pseudo Episcoporum condemnatione, qui
tunc rerum potiebantur apud Scotos, flammis olim traditus, nunc
fruitur splendore præsentiæ Christi, pro cuius gloria propagandâ nec
facultatibus nec vitæ pepercit.   Vale."

This dedication may be rendered thus :

   " *To the noble and excellent young gentleman*, JOHN WISHART *of
   the House of Pitarrow, John Gordon, a Scottish Briton,
   presents a hearty salutation.*

   "In former days, dearest Wishart, when you attended our debating
society, you discussed the religious controversies of the time, and
reviewed the arguments by which emissaries of the priesthood sought
to render attractive the foolish doctrines of the Romish Church.
These arguments, though with less ability, I have endeavoured to
expound.   And it has occurred to me to select from our theological
conversations some brief propositions ; by which, on substantial

grounds, we demonstrate that the bishops and learned men of Rome had lapsed into the degrading errors of the heathens, and of the Arians, Nestorians, and disciples of Eutychus; so that episcopal ordination, in which they rejoice, has through the corruption of their doctrines become foolish and absurd. In the present aspect of the papacy those corrupt persons have left no trace of the true Church. Through kindly feeling, and in your zeal for God's glory, you have urged me to publish these propositions; so that our youths might be fortified against papal idolatry, which is spreading everywhere, and wrecking men's souls, while dazzling them with the glare of worldly honour, and the fleeting splendour of terrestrial opulence. These propositions, originated in your own suggestions, accept, dear Wishart, so that they may profit not yourself only, but all who desire help. And in the treasury of your heart cherish, I pray you, the memory of your great paternal uncle, George Wishart; who, after faithfully upholding the cause of Christian truth against false bishops, then all-powerful in Scotland, was betrayed to the flames, and who now rejoices in the bright presence of Christ, for the maintenance of whose glorious doctrines he gave up his life."

About the year 1582, John Wishart married a daughter of Forrester of Carden, Stirlingshire—a union which, according to Scot of Scotstarvet,* was most obnoxious to his father. Of the marriage were born two children, a son and daughter. The daughter, whose Christian name was Margaret, married Sir David Lindsay of Edzell and Glenesk, who had in June 1605 a desperate encounter with his brother-in-law, the young laird of Pitarrow, at the Salt Tron of Edinburgh. They fought a whole day, and one Guthrie, a follower of Wishart, was killed, others on both sides being wounded. On account of this public outrage, the fathers of the two combatants were imprisoned by the chancellor, Archbishop Spottiswoode, for not putting restraint upon their sons.† John Wishart's son predeceased his father, unmarried. His Christian name is not certainly known.‡

* Sir John Scot records some gossip on the subject of this union, which it is undesirable to reproduce (Scot's Staggering State, ed. 1872, p. 111).

† Pitcairn's Criminal Trials, vol. iii., p. 61.

‡ The Christian name of young Wishart was William or Walter; the initials

John Wishart was, on the 30th April 1607, served heir to his father in the baronies of Pitarrow and Reidhall.* He was afterwards knighted. Having become deeply involved, he sold his estates in 1615 to his younger brother James. On this event his wife retired to England, where she was maintained by her relative, Lady Annandale.† Sir John proceeded to Ireland, where he obtained a grant of some escheated lands in county Fermanagh. Some curious details respecting his career in Ireland are supplied by Father Hay in his memoir of James Spottiswoode, Bishop of Clogher.‡ According to Hay, Sir John held "twenty-four townes or tates" of Bishop Spottiswoode's lands, for which he agreed to pay £36 of yearly rent. The rent being withheld, the bishop procured a warrant of distress, and thereupon arrested Sir John's cattle. This procedure being made public, Lord Balfour of Glenawly, a Scottish settler in the county of Fermanagh,§ to whom the bishop was obnoxious, obtained, on Sir John's behalf, letters of reprisal, and with a powerful force seized cattle belonging to the bishop. Some time afterwards the bishop's servants attempted to distrain the horses of Lord Balfour, on a claim for reset, when a scuffle ensued, in which Sir John Wemyss, Balfour's son-in-law, fell mortally wounded. By Lord Balfour, the slaughter of his relative was reported to the authorities in Dublin Castle, and the bishop was charged with manslaughter. He was tried in the Court of King's Bench in November 1626, and honourably acquitted.

From a letter of Sir John Wishart, contained in Bishop Spottiswoode's Memoirs, it would appear that Lord Balfour,

W. W., with the date 1622, are inscribed on a panel which formerly belonged to the Wishart family pew in the parish church of Fordoun (Jervise's Angus and Mearns, p. 387).

   * Inquisitiones Speciales, Kincardine, No. 21.

   † Scot's Staggering State, p. 111.

   ‡ Spottiswoode Miscellany, vol. i., pp. 110-136.

   § James Balfour, second son of Sir James Balfour of Pittendriech, and brother of the first Lord Balfour of Burley, was created, 6th July 1619, Lord Balfour, Baron of Glenawly, in the county of Fermanagh.

though retaining his hostility to the bishop, ceased to associate with Sir John. The editor of the bishop's memoirs in the *Spottiswoode Miscellany* expresses an opinion that Sir John, whose manner was boastful and absurd, suggested to Sir Walter Scott the character of Captain Craigengelt in the " Bride of Lammermoor." *

James Wishart, second son of Sir John Wishart and Jean Douglas, having acquired the lands of Pitarrow from his elder brother, had a charter thereto on the 12th December 1615. He also acquired the lands of Glenfarquhar and Monboddo. His affairs having become embarrassed, he about the year 1631 sold the lands of Pitarrow, with the lands of Carnebeg, Woodtown, and the mill of Conveth, to David, Lord Carnegie, for the sum of 59,000 merks, or £3277, 15s. 6¾d. sterling. In the instrument of sale, " Sir John Wishart, sometime of Pitarrow " is named as still living.† In a state of poverty, James Wishart proceeded to Ireland ; he became a captain in the king's service, and perished in battle. He left no male issue. His wife, Margaret Bickerton,‡ by whom he obtained a considerable fortune, survived him, and resided in Edinburgh, supported by her relations.

William, third son of Sir John Wishart of Pitarrow, and his wife, Jean Douglas, entered the University of King's College, Aberdeen, in 1606, and there graduated in 1612.§ He was admitted coadjutor in the parochial charge of Fettercairn, Kincardineshire, 24th April 1611, and was afterwards translated to Minto. He returned to Fettercairn in 1618, and was in May 1630 translated to South Leith. In 1634 he sat as a member of the Court of High Commission, and was admitted a burgess and guild-brother of Edinburgh on the 27th July 1636. As an opponent of the Covenant, he was on the 9th

* Spottiswoode Miscellany, vol. i., p. 134.

† Fraser's Earls of Southesk, p. lxvii. By the representative of Lord Carnegie, the estate of Pitarrow was sold in 1831 to Alexander Crombie of Phesdo, to whose family it still belongs.

‡ Pitarrow Writs, quoted by Mr Fraser in his " Earls of Southesk."

§ Fasti Aberdonensis.

June 1639 deposed from the pastoral office, and, having supported Charles I. in the assertion of his prerogative, was
forced to leave Scotland. He resided several years in Corn-
wall, and there died. He published in 1633 an "Exposition
of the Lord's Prayer," 18mo; and in 1642 "Immanuel," a
poem. He married Elizabeth, daughter of Alexander Keith
of Phesdo, who was served heir to her father on the 25th April
1634. Of this marriage was born a son, John, who was killed
fighting on the king's side, at the battle of Edgehill, 23d
October 1642.[*]

Alexander, fourth son of Sir John Wishart and Jean
Douglas, entered the University of King's College, Aberdeen,
in 1626. He married Catherine, daughter of the Rev. Robert
Kerr, minister of Linton, and had a son, William.

William Wishart, son of Alexander Wishart and Catherine
Kerr, graduated in the University of Edinburgh in 1645. In
August 1649, he was admitted minister of Kinneil,[†] Linlith-
gowshire. Joining the Protesters, he was a member of the
Dissenting Presbytery from the 6th August 1651 to the
11th February 1659. By the Committee of Estates, he was,
on the 15th September 1660, ordered to confine himself to his
chamber, and in other five days was committed to prison at
Edinburgh. After an imprisonment of thirteen months, partly
in Stirling Castle, he was, on the petition of the Presbytery
of Linlithgow, restored to freedom. Being sequestrated for
refusing to disown the "Remonstrance,"[‡] he was deprived of
his stipend, which, however, the Estates of Parliament, by an
Act passed on the 29th January 1661, granted to his wife.
He was intercommuned by the Privy Council on the 6th
August 1675, on the charge of keeping conventicles, or
preaching without public sanction. On the 5th February
1685, sentence of banishment to his Majesty's plantations
was pronounced against him for his refusing the Test, but he

---

[*] Scott's Fasti Eccl. Scot., vol. iii., p. 866; and vol. i., p. 99.
[†] This parish is now united to Borrowstounness.
[‡] A document addressed by the General Assembly of February 1645 to Charles I.,
reflecting on his conduct in the severest terms.

was relieved on granting a bond to appear when called upon.
He afterwards resided at Leith ; and when the Toleration
Act was passed, he ministered to a congregation in that place.
He died in February 1692, about the age of sixty-seven.[*]
He married Christian, daughter of Richard Burne, of the
family of Burne of Middlemill, Fifeshire, a magistrate of
Linlithgow. Of this marriage were born three sons—George,
James, and William.

George Wishart, eldest son of the Rev. William Wishart,
minister of Kinneil, obtained a commission in the army,
and became lieutenant-colonel of the Dragoon Guards. He
purchased the estate of Cliftonhall, Edinburghshire. A royal
warrant, dated 19th April 1700, authorised a patent to be
prepared, conferring on him, with remainder to his heirs
whomsoever, a baronetcy of Scotland. This honour was conferred on the 17th June 1706, with the limitation originally
designed. Sir George Wishart, Bart., married, as his first
wife, Anne, daughter of —— Barclay of Colairney, Fifeshire, by whom he had a daughter, Margaret, who espoused
David Stuart of Fettercairn. On the death of Sir George,
which took place prior to August 1722, her eldest son succeeded to the baronetcy of Wishart, and became known as Sir
William Stuart, Bart. This branch of the Wishart family
is now represented by Harriet Williamina, only child of the
late Sir John Hepburn-Stuart Forbes, Bart. of Pitsligo, and
wife of Baron Clinton.

Sir George Wishart, Bart., married, secondly, Fergusia
M'Cubbin, of a Galloway family, by whom he had two
daughters, Fergusia and Cordelia. By a deed of entail, dated
4th January 1718, he conveyed his estate of Cliftonhall to
himself and his heirs-male, whom failing, to his daughter Fergusia. On the death of Sir George Wishart, without heirs-
male, Fergusia Wishart expede a general service as heiress
of provision to her father, whereby she took up the unexe-
cuted procuratory of resignation, and obtained a charter
from the superior of the estate of Cliftonhall, conform to an

* Fasti Eccl. Scot., vol. i., p. 172.

instrument of sasine.* In 1727, she married George Lockhart of Carnwath, Lanarkshire. She is now represented by
Alexander Dundas Ross Wishart Baillie Cochrane of Lam-
ington, M.P. for the Isle of Wight.

Cordelia Wishart, younger daughter of Sir George Wishart,
Bart., by his second marriage, married William Sinclair of
Rosslyn ; she died without surviving issue.

James, second son of the Rev. William Wishart, minister of
Kinneil, entered the Royal Navy, and in 1703 became Admiral
of the White. In 1708, and from 1712 to 1714, he was a
Lord of the Admiralty. He commanded a fleet in the Medi-
terranean, and was knighted by Queen Anne. He died
without issue in May 1723, leaving a fortune of £20,000 to
his nephew, William Wishart, Principal of the University of
Edinburgh.

William, third son of the Rev. William Wishart, minister
of Kinneil, studied at the universities of Utrecht and Edinburgh, graduating at the latter in 1680. In 1684 he suffered
imprisonment on a charge of denying the king's authority. On
the 10th August 1691, he was ordained minister of the first
charge of Leith. His settlement was resisted by the ad-
herents of Mr Charles Kay, the non-jurant incumbent of the
second charge. On the following day he preached under the
protection of an armed "guard." He was translated to the
Tron Church, Edinburgh, in 1707, and in 1710 was appointed
Principal of the University of Edinburgh, an office he held
along with his parochial charge. He received the degree
of D.D., and was on five occasions chosen Moderator of the
General Assembly. He published two volumes of discourses,
and greatly excelled in his public ministrations. He married
Janet, daughter of Major William Murray, brother of John
Murray of Touchadam, Stirlingshire, and who on the 8th
June 1714 was served heir-portioner of her aunt, Mrs Anne
Cunningham of Drumquhassel ; she died on the 30th June
1744. Principal Wishart died on the 11th June 1729, in his

* Particular Register of Sasines, 10th December 1726.

sixty-ninth year.* He was father of two sons, William and George.

George, younger son of Principal William Wishart, studied at the University of Edinburgh, and there graduated 27th May 1719. He was in June 1726 ordained minister of St Cuthbert's, Edinburgh, and translated to the Tron Church in July 1730. By the Commission of the General Assembly he was, in 1743, appointed one of their delegates to procure an Act of Parliament for establishing the Ministers' Widows Fund. In May 1746, he was elected principal clerk of the General Assembly, and in 1748 was chosen Moderator. He received the degree of D.D. in 1759, and in 1765 was appointed chaplain in ordinary to the king, and one of the Deans of the Chapel Royal. Esteemed as a preacher, he was beloved for his amiable manners. He died 12th June 1785, aged eighty-three.† He married Anne, daughter of John Campbell of Orchard, cousin and heir of Sir James Campbell, Bart. of Ardkinglass, by whom he had, with other daughters who died unmarried, Janet, who married Major-General Beckwith, and Jane, who married the Baron von Westphalen. Dr George Wishart died 17th November 1782, aged seventy-two.

William Wishart, elder son of Principal William Wishart, studied for the Scottish Church, and began his ministry as pastor of the Presbyterian church, Founder's Hall, London. In 1737 he was presented to the New Greyfriars' church, Edinburgh, but his settlement was delayed consequent on a charge of heresy being brought against him by the Presbytery, of which he was acquitted by the General Assembly. He was, in 1737, appointed Principal of the University of Edinburgh, and in 1745 was elected Moderator of the General Assembly. He published sermons and essays, and edited various theological works. He married first, in December 1724, Margaret, daughter of Professor Thomas Haliburton of St Andrews, and by her, who died 27th February 1746, had

* Fasti Eccl. Scot., vol. i., pp. 56, 101. † Ib., pp. 56, 121.

G

a son, William Thomas; another son, who died in January
1739; and three daughters—Anne, who died in 1819, aged
eighty-two; Janet, who married Mr Maxwell, merchant,
Dundee; and Margaret, who married James Macdowall,
merchant, Edinburgh. Principal Wishart married, secondly,
on the 17th March 1747, Frances, daughter of James Deans
of Woodhouselee. He died 12th May 1753. His widow
married Dr John Scot of Stewartfield, and subsequently John
Struther Ker of Littledean, Roxburghshire.*

William Thomas Wishart, only surviving son of Principal
William Wishart, possessed the estate of Foxhall, in the
county of Linlithgow. He was, on the 30th March 1768,
served heir to his father in the estate of Carsebonny, Stirlingshire. He recorded his arms † 22d February 1769, as only
son of Principal Wishart, and was allowed supporters as heir-
male of Pitarrow. He married, in April 1768, Anne, eldest
daughter of George Balfour, Writer to the Signet, and died
3d December 1799, leaving five sons, William, George,
Patrick, Archibald, and John Henry.

William, eldest son of William Thomas Wishart of Foxhall
and Carsebonny, succeeded his father. He was major in the
15th Regiment of Foot, and died unmarried on the 14th
August 1805. On his death the representation of the House
of Pitarrow devolved on his brother George; but the family
estates passed by settlement to his next brother, Patrick.
George Wishart was served heir-male of Sir George Wishart,
Bart., before the Sheriff of Edinburgh, 18th July 1843, and
assumed the baronetcy under the erroneous belief that it was
destined to heirs-male. He died unmarried before 1860.

Patrick, third son of William Thomas Wishart, was a Writer
to the Signet. He sold the family estates. By his wife, Margaret, daughter of Alexander Robertson of Prenderguest, Ber-
wickshire, he had three sons, William Thomas, James, and
Alexander, and three daughters, Philadelphia-Anne, Hope-
Balfour, and Jane. William Thomas, the eldest son, took orders
in the English Church; he died at St John, New Brunswick,

* Fasti Eccl. Scot., vol. i., pp. 59, 70.   † Lyon Register.

without issue. The two younger sons died unmarried. Philadelphia-Anne, the eldest daughter, married Dr Macnider ; and Jane, the third daughter, married Major-General W. J Gairdner, C.B., Bengal Army, by whom she had Archie Wishart Gairdner, lieutenant 109th Regiment, George Gairdner, in the service of the Hudson Bay Company, James Gairdner, R.N., and others.

Archibald, fourth son of William Thomas Wishart, was a Writer to the Signet, and keeper of the Register of Sasines. He married, but died childless.

John Henry, the fifth son, practised as a surgeon in Edinburgh. He married Louisa, daughter of Major Wilson, R.A., by Martha, daughter of Robert White, M.D., of Bennochy, Fifeshire, and left three sons and two daughters. William, the eldest son, died in India ; the second son, James, was a surgeon in the army, and died at Scutari in 1856. John, the third son, male representative of the House of Wishart of Pitarrow, is now resident in Australia.

Adam Wishart, third son of John Wishart, Sheriff of the Mearns or Kincardineshire, obtained, in 1272, a charter of the lands of Ballandarg and Logie, and in 1279 a charter of the lands of Kenny Murchardyn, or Kennyneil, all in the county of Forfar.* Gilbert, eldest son of Adam Wishart, swore fealty to Edward I. at Elgin on the 24th July 1296.† Robert, the second son, was advanced from the office of Archdeacon of Lothian to the Bishopric of Glasgow in 1272, when William Wishart of that see was postulated to St Andrews. According to the Chartulary of Melrose he was consecrated at Aberdeen on Sunday before the Feast of the Purification, 1272. He was a Privy Councillor of Alexander III., and on the death of that monarch in 1285 was appointed a Lord of Regency. So long as Edward I. evinced a desire to uphold the independence of Scotland, Bishop Wishart gave him countenance. But when the abdication of Baliol revealed the duplicity of the English monarch, he attached

* Dalrymple's Historical Collections, 217 ; Reg. Vet. de Aberd., 332.
† Ragman Roll, p. 146.

himself to the patriotic party, and in 1297 joined the standard
of Wallace. Though a churchman, he assumed the coat of
mail, and performed military duties in the field.

When Robert the Bruce resolved to assert his right to the
Scottish throne in the spring of 1306, Bishop Wishart gave
him a cordial support, and at his coronation, which took
place at Scone on the 27th March, he, in absence of the
regalia, which Edward had removed to London, supplied
from his own wardrobe the robes in which King Robert
appeared on the occasion. He was present with his sovereign
at the battle of Methven, fought on the 18th of June. This
engagement having resulted disastrously, Bishop Wishart
sought shelter in the castle of Cupar-Fife. There he fell into
the hands of the invaders, and being bound in chains, was
sent as a prisoner to England. Confined in the castle of
Nottingham, he was subjected to much indignity, and
narrowly escaped death. He was afterwards detained in
Porchester Castle, and the Pope was entreated to make
vacant his see and to appoint as his successor a bishop
favourable to the English interests.*

After the decisive battle of Bannockburn, Bishop Wishart
was, along with Bruce's wife, daughter, sister, and nephew,
exchanged for the Earl of Hereford, who had been made a
prisoner by the Scots. During his long confinement he had endured many privations, and become blind. He died on the 26th
November 1316, and his remains were deposited in his cathedral church.† During his episcopate, he forwarded the erection
of his cathedral. It was alleged by Edward I. that he used
timber, allowed him for erecting a steeple to his cathedral, in
constructing instruments of war for the reduction of Kirkin-
tilloch Peel, held by the English.‡

John Wishart, nephew of Bishop Robert Wishart, and prob-

* Rymer's Fœdera, vol. i., part ii., new ed., p. 996; Prynne; Edward I.,
p. 1156; Tytler's History of Scotland, Edin., 1869, 12mo, vol. i., pp. 89, 94.

† History of Glasgow, edited by the Rev. J. S. Gordon, D.D., Glasg., 1871,
p. 53.

‡ Burton's History of Scotland, Edin., 1873, vol. iii., p. 429; Innes's Sketches
of Early Scottish History, Edin., 1861, p. 50.

ably a younger son of Gilbert Wishart of Logie, was sometime Archdeacon of Glasgow. In this capacity he vigorously
upheld the national cause, but was unhappily taken prisoner
by Edward II., who, on the 6th April 1310, ordered his
removal from the castle of Conway to the city of Chester, and
from thence to the Tower of London. Released after the
battle of Bannockburn, he resumed his duties as archdeacon.
In 1319 he was appointed Bishop of Glasgow. He died in
1325.[*]

To the family of Ballandarg and Logie probably belonged
John Wyshert, who, on the 12th April 1378, received from the
Privy Council of England a passport, authorising him to proceed from Scotland to the University of Oxford for the pur-
poses of study.[†]

Alexander Wishart was, in 1409, member of an inquest
respecting the lands of Meikle Kenny, in the parish of Kingoldrum, Forfarshire. In a charter of these lands, granted by
Malcolm, Abbot of Arbroath, in 1466, is named John, son of
John Wishart of Logie.[‡]

In 1526 John Wishart succeeded his father Alexander in
the lands of Kennyneil.[§] On the 22d October 1530, he obtained a precept of a charter of the lands of Logie Wishart,
Ballandarg Wester, and others.[||] He had, on the 30th Janu-
ary 1531, a letter of regress of the lands of Lokarstoun and
others.[¶] On the 31st July 1538, a protection was granted by
James V. to John Wishart of Logie Wishart, and Christian
Ogilvy, his spouse, with John, Alexander, Katherine, and
Christian Wishart, their sons and daughters, and William
Wishart, brother to the said John, and to their lands and
goods.[**]

On the forfeiture of Archibald, Earl of Angus, superior
of Logie Wishart, John Wishart resigned his lands to
James V., from whom, on the 29th May 1540, he received

---

* Gordon's History of Glasgow, p. 58. † Rotuli Scotiæ, vol. ii., p. 8*.
‡ Reg. Nig. de Aberd., pp. 47, 50. § Ib.
|| Reg. Sec. Sig., vol. viii., fol. 195. ¶ Ib., vol. ix., fol. 72.
** Ib., vol. xii., fol. 6.

a charter of the lands of Logie Wishart and others.* He
further obtained a royal charter, erecting his whole lands into
a barony, to be styled "the barony of Wishart," and a letter,
dated 14th October 1540, whereby the king's right to the said
barony was discharged.† This branch of the House of Wishart
became henceforth known as the Wisharts of that ilk.

Alexander Strachan, son of John Wishart of Logie Wishart
(named in the protection of James V.), died in November
1569, leaving three daughters—Margaret, Isobel, and Janet.
By his will, which was confirmed in the Commissary Court of
Edinburgh, on the 6th April 1570, he appointed his brother
George Wishart tutor to his daughters.‡

George Wishart, a younger son of John Wishart of Logie
Wishart, became a burgess of Dundee, and engaged in
merchandise in that place. In the burgh records of Dundee
"George Vischart" appears eighth in a list of sixteen coun-
cillors, dated 28th September 1550. He is, on the 24th September 1553, entered last on a list of four bailies. In the
Record of the Convention of Royal Burghs,§ held at Dundee
on the 28th September 1555, he is named as one of the commissioners of that burgh. He continued to act as a magistrate in the Burgh Court till 1564.

On the 28th October 1563, George Wishart obtained a precept of a charter, confirming him in the superiority lands of
Kirriemuir, granted to him by his father, "John Wishart of that
ilk." || On the 27th January 1554-5, he granted a discharge
to his brother, John Wishart of that ilk, for five hundred
merks, in satisfaction of his claim on half the lands of Ballandarg.¶ By a royal letter, dated at Stirling, 7th March 1568,
he received a gift of all the goods which belonged to James
Cramond of Auldbar, which had become escheat by his being
denounced rebel.

* Reg. Sec. Sig., vol. xiii., fol. 93.
† Ib., vol. xiv., fol. 52b; Acta Parl. Scot., vol. ii., p. 379.
‡ Edinburgh Com. Reg., Testaments, vol. ii.
§ Record of Convention of Royal Burghs, Edin., 1866, 4to, vol. i., p. 10.
|| Reg. Sec. Sig., vol. xxxii., p. 114.
¶ Wedderburn's Protocols in the Town-Clerk's Office, Dundee.

John Wishart of Logie Wishart died in the year 1574. By his will, dated 2d September 1574, he appointed Marion Gardyne, his spouse, and Thomas Wishart, his second son, his executors, with Patrick Ogilvy of Inchmartin as "oversman." To his daughter Euphan he bequeathed £500; he also made a provision for his daughters, Mirabell, Agnes, and Katherine.*

John Wishart, the next baron of Logie Wishart, obtained the honour of knighthood. He had two sons, John and Gilbert, and one daughter. Gilbert Wishart was, on the 30th November 1614, denounced rebel for non-payment of a debt of eighty pounds Scots.†

On the 30th October 1629, John Wishart of that ilk was served heir to his uncle, in lands situated in the regality of Kirriemuir ; also to his father, Sir John Wishart, in the lands of Kennyneil.‡ He seems to have died unmarried.

Thomas Wishart, probably the same as is described as "his second son" by John Wishart of Logie Wishart, who died in 1574, obtained a portion of the lands of Inglistoun, in the county of Forfar. On the 11th January 1612, Thomas Wishart "in Ballindarg" was served heir to his father in a fourth part of the lands of Inglistoun.§ He married‖ the only daughter of Sir John Wischart of Logie Wishart, and on the death of his brother John, succeeded to the representation of the House. But the estates were dissipated. Of the marriage of Thomas Wishart "in Ballindarg" with his cousin, a daughter of Sir John Wischart of that ilk, were born two sons, George¶ and Gilbert. George Wishart was born about the year 1599. Having prosecuted his theological studies at the University of Edinburgh, and obtained licence as a probationer, he was in 1624 admitted minister of the parish

* Edinburgh Com. Reg., *Testaments*, vol. iii.

† Reg. Sec. Sig.

‡ Inq. Spec. Forfar, Nos. 188, 189.   § *Ib.*, No. 76.

‖ Genealogical MS. in the Lyon Office.

¶ Though the statement in the text as to the Bishop George Wishart's descent seems justified by the authority of Nisbet, we are only certain that the Bishop sprung from the House of Logie Wishart.

of Monifieth, Forfarshire. In 1626 he was translated to the
second charge of St Andrews. Having retired to England in
1637, he was deposed for deserting his charge. Soon afterwards he was appointed lecturer in All Saints church, Newcastle, and in 1640 was presented to St Nicholas church in
the same town. Of this latter charge he was deprived by the
House of Commons in June 1642. When the Scots took
Newcastle in October 1644, he was made prisoner, and
on the charge of corresponding with Royalists, was committed to the prison of Edinburgh, and there confined
in a felon's cell. On his petition, the Estates of Parliament, in January 1645, agreed to support his wife and
five children. When the Marquis of Montrose arrived in
Edinburgh with his victorious army, he was liberated, after
a captivity of seven months. By the Marquis he was appointed his private chaplain, and in this capacity he accompanied his benefactor both at home and abroad. At Paris,
in 1647, he published a narrative of the Marquis's exploits
under the following title :

" J. G. De rebus auspiciis serenissimi et potentissimi Caroli, Dei
gratia, Magnæ Britanniæ Regis, &c., sub imperio illustrissimi Jacobi
Montisrosarum Marchionis, Cometis de Kincardin, &c., supremi
Scotiæ gubernatoris, anno MDCXLIV. et duobus sequentibus, præ-
clare gestis, commentarius."

Wishart subsequently added a second part, bringing the
narrative down to the period of Montrose's death. A copy
of the work was suspended round Montrose's neck during his
execution.

After the fall of Montrose, Wishart became chaplain to
a Scottish regiment in the United Provinces ; he subsequently
officiated as chaplain to Elizabeth, Queen of Bohemia. On
the Restoration, he was appointed rector of Newcastle, and
on 3d June 1662 was consecrated Bishop of Edinburgh. He
died in August 1671, in his seventy-second year. Though a
vigorous upholder of the royal prerogative, he was privately a
lover of toleration. To the prisoners captured at the engage-

ment at Pentland in 1666, and warded in prison at Edinburgh, he sent daily a portion of his dinner. He bequeathed to the poor of Holyrood £500 Scots.* On an elegant mural monument raised to his memory in the Abbey of Holyrood is the following inscription:

" Hic recubat celebris Doctor Sophocardius alter,
　Entheus ille Σοφωσ καρδιαν Agricola.
　Orator fervore pio, facundior olim
　Doctiloque rapiens pectora dura modis.
　Ternus ut Antistes Wischeart, ita ternus Edinen.
　Candoris columen nobile, semper idem.
　Plus octogenis hinc gens Sophocardia lustris,
　Summis hic mitris claruit, atque tholis ;
　Dum cancellarius regni Sophocardius, idem
　Præsul erat Fani, Regulæ Sanctæ, tui.
　Atque ubi pro regno, ad Norham, contendit avito
　Brussius, indomita mente manuque potens ;
　Glasguus Robertus erat Sophocardius alter,
　Pro patria, qui se fortiter opposuit.
　Nec pacis studiis Gulielmo, animisve Roberto,
　Agricola inferior, cætera forte prior ;
　Excelsus sine fastu animus, sine fraude benignus,
　Largus opis miseris, intemerata fides.
　Attica rara fides ; constantia raraque, nullis
　Expugnata, licet mille petita, malis.
　In regem, obsequii exemplar, civisque fidelis
　Antiquam venerans, cum probitate, fidem.
　Omnibus exutum ter, quem proscriptio, carcer,
　Exilium, lustris non domuere tribus.
　Ast reduci Carolo plaudunt ubi regna secundo,
　Doctori Wischeart insula plaudit ovans.
　Olim ubi captivus, squalenteque carcere læsus,
　Annos ter ternos, præsul honorus obit.
　Vixit Olympiadas terquinas ; Nestoris annos
　Vovit Edina : obitum Scotia moesta dolet.
　Gestaque Montrosei, Latio celebrata cothurno :
　Quantula (proh) tanti sunt monumenta viri ! "

* Fasti Eccl. Scot., vol. i., p. 392 ; vol. ii., p. 394 ; vol. iii., p. 724.

Bishop Wishart's epitaph may be thus rendered in a free translation :

" Here rest the remains of the distinguished Doctor George Wishart, the third bishop of his name. Gifted with superior wisdom and piety, he by his eloquence and learning moved the stubborn and reclaimed the vicious. A pattern of honour, he maintained a consistent and upright life. For four hundred years, the members of his House were remarkable both in Church and State. William Wishart was Chancellor of the kingdom and Bishop of St Andrews. Robert Wishart was Bishop of Glasgow, and a zealous supporter of King Robert the Bruce, and an upholder of the national cause. Bishop George equalled Bishop William in his love of peace, and Bishop Robert in his patriotic valour. He celebrated the exploits of the great Montrose. In his deportment, dignity was unallied with pride. The poor shared largely of his bounty. His generous emotions neither misplaced confidence nor misfortune might arrest or overcome. Loyal to his sovereign, he was devoted to his country. Thrice deprived of his substance, he faithfully endured impeachment, imprisonment, and exile. Having long suffered adversity, he was privileged on the restoration of monarchy to experience comfort. In the city where he was cruelly imprisoned, he was for nine years an honoured bishop. He attained the venerable age of [seventy-two]. Edinburgh wished that he might reach the years of Nestor, and Scotland bewailed his death."

Bishop Wishart married Margaret Ogilvy, by whom he had four sons, Hugo, Captain James, Patrick, and Robert, and two daughters, Jean and Margaret. Jean, the elder daughter, married William Walker.*

Gilbert Wishart, younger son of Thomas Wishart in Ballandarg, graduated at King's College, Aberdeen, in 1622. Prior to the 17th March 1635, he was admitted to the pastoral charge of Dunnichen, Forfarshire. He died in January 1688, aged about eighty-six, leaving a son, John, and a daughter, Isobel, who married John Ogilvie in Easter Idvie.†

John Wishart was Regent of Philosophy in the University of Edinburgh, and one of the Commissaries of Edinburgh.

---

* Fasti Eccl. Scot., vol. i., p. 392.   † Ib., vol. ii., p. 768.

He owned the estate of Balgavie, which he latterly exchanged for the barony of Logie Wishart.* He is described by Nisbet as "nephew to the bishop, and great-grandson of Sir John Wishart of Logie." †

In the beginning of the sixteenth century or earlier, a branch of the House of Pitarrow obtained the lands of Drymme or Drum, near Montrose. In an instrument dated 14th June 1565, seising George Wishart, brother of John Wishart of Pitarrow, in the lands of Westerdoid, Forfarshire, George Wishart of Drymme is named as his attorney.‡ To the discharge of an assignation by the laird of Dun, dated 17th June 1581, George Wischart of Drimme is a witness.§ On the 7th June 1580, George Hepburn, Chancellor of Brechin, directed to him as bailie a precept of sasine for infefting Paul Fraser, precentor of Brechin, in a portion of waste land. ‖

To George Wishart, elder of Drymme, was granted on the 7th August 1591, a royal charter of the moor called Menboy.¶ By George Wishart of Drymme, son of the preceding, the moor of Menboy was, on the 26th July 1605, sold to Alexander Campbell, Bishop of Brechin, and Helen Clephane, his second wife.**

Of the family of Wishart of Drum, certain members settled in the parish and burgh of Montrose. In the parish register of Montrose, "George Wyscheart, guidman of Irvine," is, on the 22d October 1624, named as witness to a baptism. *Bailie* George Wyschart is mentioned in the baptismal register on the 22d March of the same year. On the 2d March 1649, James Wischart, described as lawful son of Mr James Wischart, burgess of Montrose, had sasine of a tenement in Brechin as nearest of kin to Thomas Ramsay of Brechin, notary public, his uncle.†† In 1656 James Wischeart is named as a member of the town council of

* Genealogical MS. in the Lyon Office, p. 477.
† Nisbet's System of Heraldry, vol. i., p. 201.
‡ Protocol Book of Thomas Ireland in the Town-Clerk's Office, Dundee.
§ Reg. Episc. Brechin., p. 309, No. 272. ‖ *Ib.*, p. 215, No. 193.
¶ *Ib.*, p. 286, No. 246. ** *Ib.*, p. 292, No. 253. †† *Ib.*, p. 247, No. 189.

Montrose, and on the 28th October of the same year, Mr
James Wishart, a son of the preceding, was chosen "doctor"
or rector of the grammar school.

Mr James Wishart, rector of the grammar school of
Montrose, was father of a son, William, and three daughters,
Jean, Margaret, and Elizabeth.   He died 11th September
1683.*   William Wishart studied at the University of Edinburgh, and was, on the 23d April 1669, ordained by George
Wishart, Bishop of Edinburgh, minister of Newabbey.   He
was, in 1680, translated to Wamphray, where he died
unmarried in February 1685.

Elizabeth, third daughter of Mr James Wishart, born
November 1664, married Robert Strachan, rector of the
grammar school of Montrose, descended from the ancient
House of Strachan of Thornton, Kincardineshire. †

By patent, dated 22d February 1769, the arms of William
Thomas Wishart, head and representative of the House of
Pitarrow, were recorded in the Lyon Register: *argent*, three
piles or passion nails, meeting in a point, *gules ; supporters*—
two horses, *argent*, saddled and bridled, *gules ; crest*—a demi-
eagle, wings expanded, proper.

* Fasti Eccl. Scot., vol. i., pp. 507, 664 ; Montrose Parish Records.
† Montrose Parish Records.

INDEX.

THE END.

M'Farlane & Erskine, Printers, Edinburgh.